SALLY
FORTH

SALLY
FORTH

Ian Paterson

THOROGOOD

Published by Thorogood
10-12 Rivington Street
London EC2A 3DU
Telephone: 020 7749 4748
Email: info@thorogoodpublishing.co.uk
Web: www.thorogoodpublishing.co.uk

A CIP catalogue record for this book is available from the British Library.

ISBN paperback: 978 191492801 7
ISBN e-book: 978 191492802 4

For Linda

1.

SALLY FORTH

Had she married him, she would have been called *'Sally Forth'*.

Although his surname was never hers, she had begun to use it early on in their short relationship, and she had employed it thereafter whenever she signed up for a store discount card or volunteered for a focus group. It had been one of her most cherished possessions, although it must be said she did not, at the time, have many.

How strange it was that she had not yet completely abandoned it. Despite Tony Forth having left her without any ceremony, her attachment to the name seemed to grow. It was as if she could not completely accept closure of that abject period of her life for which Tony Forth was responsible.

Standing there in the queue that miserably-wet November evening, pondering on her future, she slipped again into musing on her many mistakes of the past. She wondered, for the first time and rather whimsically, whether she had perhaps contemplated getting married to Tony Forth merely for his name; after all, there had not been much else he could have offered her. However, as much as she regretted their relationship, she immediately berated herself for entertaining that notion – it was unfair both to Tony and to herself, since at one time while they had been together they had experienced a real affection for each other.

Yet, she knew that she was deluding herself and, most certainly, that he, too, had been deluding her.

She decided that this was not a topic in which she should engage further, because she knew how morose it made her.

In any event, Sally had been eager to rid herself of the name 'Sally Bridge'. She had on countless occasions, whether by way of a genuine mishearing or a facile joke made at her expense, been asked whether what she was saying was that her name

2

was 'Stalybridge', alluding to the small town near to Ashton-under-Lyne where she had grown up. Getting rid of her given name was not merely Sally's aim – it had become an imperative, so tired was she of it.

She began to reflect on how she might achieve that objective. She could have done so simply by way of deed poll or by marrying Tony Forth – but only if she avoided a double-barrelled surname, since 'Sally Forth-Bridge' would defeat the whole purpose.

Changing her name was one thing. What about also changing her *address*? Sally was fed up with having to explain, time and time again, that underlining *'Ashton'* was not what she meant when she gave her address as 'Ashton-under-Lyne' – the only town she knew with an *'under-Lyne'*. She thought that it must be just as bad for punctilious punctuationalists living in Westward Ho!, the only town in the UK with an exclamation mark as part of its adopted name.

Sally found it difficult to change the subject – it kept dropping back into her inbox. She had had to admit to herself that her wanting to marry Tony might, to some exceedingly small extent, have been influenced by her pre-occupation with playing with names. This thought frightened her. She was an educated woman and to think that she could have allowed her sense of playfulness to influence one of life's most significant decisions made her wonder whether she really knew herself.

And then, at last, she was able to move on and to contemplate something else.

She tried to remember the word given to the idea that some people appear to gravitate towards jobs suggested by their names, like a person with the surname *'Weed'* becoming President of The Royal Horticultural Society. Maybe, she thought, the theory also extended to our personal traits; after all, some dog owners come to look like their pets. Or was it the other way around? Then it came to her from nowhere – the name is *'nominative determinism'* or something of the sort.

She had now been waiting forty-five minutes to see the Manager and the delay was beginning to upset her.

She knew that she was almost certainly wasting her time, but she would give it just another quarter of an hour before giving up. In truth, however, there was no one waiting anywhere for *her* and little reason for her to hurry back home other than to avoid the indignity of being kept waiting – and it certainly was an indignity to be kept waiting overlong. She thought about the fact that people are often kept waiting in a queue longer than necessary by way of encouragement to leave it, which, she felt, was quite ridiculous. That is certainly what happens with most of the telephone calls she made to call centres; they should begin to show a bit of honesty by playing messages along the lines of *"We are sorry for the delay in answering your call, but we are busy at this present time. Your call **is** important to us, so please stay on the line until it eventually ceases to be important to **you**."*

Suddenly, as if in corroboration, a young girl ahead of Sally in the queue shook her head in disgust and went off in a huff, striding forcefully through the swing doors, thus enabling the line of impatients to inch forward – Sally with it.

As she shuffled forward, she caught sight of a poster on the wall advertising the upcoming *'Alice's Adventures in Wonderland'*, which triggered a thought of her twin sister, Alice. She reflected on how their close ties had nearly become much looser but that now they were even tighter than they had been during their childhood. She knew that, without Alice, her world would have collapsed. She owed much to her.

Sally reverted to what she enjoyed doing most when she needed to kill time – playing with words and with names. Occupying herself with such diversions was not something Sally would indulge only when she was bored – she regarded it as a leisure activity for every occasion.

As for names, she could not converse with anyone – adult or child – unless she knew what they called themselves. It was as if she needed permission or a kind of password to enable her to open a door to their soul or, if such grand a thing as their soul was not on offer, to open the door to a meaningful exchange rather than to some idle banter.

She was aware that other people in the queue might feel it unnatural to remain in close proximity to another mortal for more than five minutes without striking up some kind of conversation or, at least, acknowledging their existence in some way and that instead of playing word games she should find solace in chatting to a fellow waiter-in-line. However, although Sally was more than adept at making casual conversation, she much preferred her own company. Making new friends had never exactly been her speciality.

Wordplay was, indeed, her favourite diversion – she could not look at any word of more than five letters without working out how it would read backwards or whether it could be manipulated into a fitting anagram.

She glanced at the door ahead on which she saw a scruffy old sign – *'Manager'* – and underneath it a pristine, newly-affixed, blue plastic nameplate with white edging, announcing *'Simon D Leigh'*. This, she thought, had a useful collection of letters to create an anagram. She started with three letters, *I N* and *G*, and by shuffling around the remaining eight – *S, M, O, D, L, E, I* and *H* – she soon came up with the anagram *'demolishing'*. She hoped that if it had any validity the theory of nominative determinism had no application to Simon D Leigh.

2.

TWINS

Alice was the elder twin. Their parents had told them that this accident of primogeniture was a matter of no more than ten minutes so that nothing should ever turn on it.

In practice, however, Alice was always relying on this to resolve their disagreements; to determine little issues of doubt between them; to fix Sally with an irksome chore about the house which she did not want to do or to allow her to claim ownership of the last chocolate biscuit in the packet. By and large, Sally accepted this. She did not mind being put upon, and she treated these inconveniences merely as an inevitable consequence of being the second born. Of course, those mere ten minutes constituted an entirely illogical basis for such serfdom, although it would take Sally many years to realise that.

In school, Alice and Sally would not be parted from each other and in consequence they had few friends and certainly no close friends. Had their parents in a casual conversation raised the issue or had they invited any of their classmates home for tea, then both Alice and Sally might have realised that it was possibly a good idea for the girls not to rely entirely on friendship with each other. For a start, learning how to make and keep friends is one of life's great pleasures – one which neither of them picked up or even realised that they had **not** picked up.

That knack is like learning a foreign language, an endeavour which is much easier to acquire in early life than in adulthood. With kids, there is no artifice in striking up a conversation with another child. When we are young, the transition in friendship from stranger to best friend can be instantaneous and seamless but we do not have to advance very far in age to recognise the impediments which all but the most uninhibited of us will experience as adults in forging new relationships. Many of those impediments are imposed by society, of which young children are fortunately oblivious.

The idea of making other friends would have been difficult for their parents to propose to twins who loved each other unconditionally and who would suffer if anything were to come between them.

Thus, even more difficult would it have been to tell the girls (or even to hint to them) that they might not always be each other's best friend and that they should therefore take out 'insurance' by cultivating a friend or two.

Sally knew, however, that a small dose of cynicism administered with love and with care would have been better than the pill which they both had had to swallow when trying to make friends as adults.

◆ ◆ ◆

To celebrate the twenty-fifth anniversary of the creation of Greater Manchester (within which the Metropolitan Borough of Oldham sits), scholarships were created to allow fifteen talented students, who would not otherwise have been able to afford it, entry to fee-paying grammar schools. Their parents had heard about this early on and did everything they could to give Sally and Alice the extra coaching necessary to achieve scholarships.

The joy on that Saturday when a letter advising the Bridges that Sally had been awarded a scholarship to Oldham Independent School was completely neutralised by the lack of a similar acceptance letter for Alice. Sally wanted to celebrate but could not bring herself to do so. The atmosphere in the Bridge household had been completely blighted, since everyone had assumed that, if **both** girls had managed to get in, then that would have been conveyed to their parents in the same letter.

Throughout that weekend, their parents had moped around the house in silent bewilderment as to how to handle the situation. Sally thought that anything she said would appear triumphant; and Alice – well, Alice was beyond despair. She felt she had lost not only her twin sister but also her one opportunity to succeed in life. She resented Sally for being the lucky one – and the cleverer one.

It was, however, the mechanics of post office letter-sorting combined with the whimsy of the postal delivery service which were to blame – not Alice's inadequacy – because the letter confirming the award of **her** scholarship arrived in the post on the Monday. By then it had become too late for a fitting celebration and what should have been the occasion for a gala ball turned out to be a perfunctory family gathering round the kitchen table with a bottle of Lucozade for which no one could muster any enthusiasm. Anguish and resentment even when washed down with joy still left a bitter taste for Alice.

These events contributed to the Bridge family never again undertaking any joint family venture other, that is, than the two short summer holidays they took in Llandudno in 1999 and 2001.

On the plus side, Alice and Sally both attended Oldham Independent School for Girls. They studied together and played together. They planned together and they hoped together. Nothing occurred in the life of one that was not known to the other. When one felt pain so did the other. They were, after all, identical twins.

What would have happened to the girls had only one of them succeeded in obtaining entry to Oldham Independent School? This was a frightening conjecture for their parents. They knew, of course, that there would always be a risk of only one twin succeeding, however, they had never gone on to ask themselves whether, if one of the girls had been cleverer than the other, it would have been fair for the cleverer to have to forego the chance of applying for a scholarship merely to save the other's self-esteem.

3.

GRANDMOTHER

Some two years before Alice and Sally had been born, an event occurred which would not come to Sally's attention for another twenty-three years. That was as well because had the bald facts been known to Sally while she was growing up as a contented twin sister, a serious split would have occurred between the two girls wide enough for them to despair of it ever being fixed. In the event, Sally was able, in blissful ignorance, to enjoy harmonious sisterly relations with Alice for some years yet.

The circumstances in question are not complex, although it is difficult to make sense of them for reasons which will become clear. Mrs Bridge's parents, Max and Julia Imber, were living and working in Whitehaven in Cumbria but had done much more working than living. Mr Imber worked every shift available as a foreman in a Whitehaven chemicals factory and Mrs Imber toiled daily as a housekeeper in the large Victorian house occupied by the owner of the factory, his wife, their five daughters and two sons.

The Imbers' hard work had enabled them, from a standing start, to buy a small, terraced property in Lowca, Whitehaven, which Mr Imber insisted should be in Mrs Imber's name, although that is not of any moment here.

In their back yard they kept chickens, tomatoes and out of the way.

Mr Imber died on 27 July 1985, aged sixty.

Mrs Imber had looked after the house and fed the chickens but relied heavily on her husband for everything else – particularly since her hearing was not too good. Above all, her husband had been her confidant in all things. The blow of losing one's loved-one is hard enough but even harder if your loved-one was the only person in whom you ever could truly confide.

Mrs Imber became a detached soul who did not talk much or go out for walks or speak to her neighbours other, that is, than the lady who lived two doors up the street with whom Mrs Imber often shared her hens' eggs in exchange for guidance when things got particularly confusing.

For the whole 20 years of their friendship Mrs Imber had called her neighbour *'Nita'* although her name was really *'Rita'*.

Not once during that time had Rita corrected her neighbour's mistaken understanding. Out of politeness, Rita had been reluctant to point out the failing of such a dear friend, besides which there had never appeared the right occasion to correct something which Rita was aware should have been put right at their first meeting.

Mrs Imber was short, buxom and determined. She had a round head with a surfeit of grey hair, which she wore plastered over her head like a swim cap. Whenever she went to visit Rita, she would sit in her parlour with her coat on, her arms positioned on her lap clutching her superannuated handbag which always contained a hard-boiled egg wrapped in greaseproof paper. Indeed, she would never venture out without a hard-boiled egg in her handbag. It was just one of those strange things which is difficult to understand.

She read (mainly detective novels) and liked to listen to classical music on the wireless.

After her husband's death, Mrs Imber had felt upset that he had not made any effort to leave her a Will (although it hardly mattered in her case). She had completely forgotten about that upset until ten months later, when she was spurred on by an item in the local newspaper to make her own Will. Fired with single-minded purpose, Mrs Imber impetuously decided that she would neither make the same mistake nor incur solicitor's fees in the process.

And so, after a chat with Rita one Sunday afternoon, Mrs Imber immediately went back home and prepared a short Will, which she wrote out on the page immediately following her bespattered recipe for tomato soup and rice. Rita's son, Tom, had warned Mrs Imber that she needed two witnesses and so that evening Mrs Imber went back to Rita's and signed her Will in front of Rita and her son in conformity with all legal requirements, if not in conformity with the usual format for a Will or with what one would expect to be the normal and sensible disposition of one's estate. It could have been a recipe for disaster.

Mrs Imber's homemade Will, dated 2nd November 1985, simply left her house in Lowca to *'my first grandchild when he/she becomes 21'*. That, of course, was the event which Sally would have complaint of.

The only 'codicil' to Mrs Imber's Will consisted of a telephone conversation, some two years later, when Mrs Imber had told her daughter that since she already owned a home it would be "*wasteful*" for her to inherit the house in Cumbria.

"And by the way, it's about time you settled down and had a child."

This injunction was made regularly by Mrs Imber to little good effect. Her daughter merely listened with a wry smile and said nothing.

The cost of the upkeep of her house in Lowca was beginning to concern Mrs Imber, for although she continued to work as a housekeeper, she nevertheless struggled to pay the household bills. Furthermore, her health being questionable, Mrs Imber spent a lot of time worrying about whether it was sensible for her to live so far apart from her only daughter.

Whilst Mrs Imber delighted in the peace of the countryside and the taste of the sea, she had not, even after her husband's death, formed any local friendships or attachments apart from with Rita and so when in 1991 the invitation came to move to Ashton-under-Lyne to live with her daughter's family, her acceptance followed quickly. All previous reservations concerning living with her daughter and son-in-law had, by then, been either forgotten or overlooked. It would, nonetheless, be a wrench for Mrs Imber to leave for at no time since Mr and Mrs Imber had come to live in Lowca had either of them ventured more than three miles away except, that is, for their honeymoon in Gretna which was no more than fifty miles away. They had become as much wedded to their beloved home in Lowca as they were to each other.

Mrs Imber was uncertain as to what she would do about the house once she had moved to Ashton-under-Lyne and so she relied, once again, on Rita's invaluable advice. Rita's son was looking for a house for his newly-acquired family of three and there could be no one more reliable than Tom to act as the custodian of Mrs Imber's property. They agreed a weekly rental to start immediately from the day after Mrs Imber was to leave Lowca.

On moving day – a very moving day – her daughter and son-in-law had come to collect her in their car. There was no need for a removal van since Mrs Imber had little more than a small suitcase of clothes to bring with her. Her departure would have looked to anyone as if she were off on her holidays had the farewell from Rita and her son not been so emotional. Although no mention of it was made, Rita knew that she was not likely to see her friend again. Rita, too, was not well-travelled – her longest trip away from home had been to Whitehaven, less than three miles away.

The last few years of Sally's grandmother's life, although spent cossetted in the Bridge family home in Ashton-under-Lyne, were lived in decline. Mrs Imber was exhibiting unwellness, but the symptoms were different on each successive visit to her GP; he thus found her illness difficult to diagnose, particularly because she refused to undergo anything as invasive as a blood test. In consequence, she migrated from one pill to the next without any improvement to her health – or to that of her GP.

Mrs Imber's unhappy situation was compounded by two associated conditions – acute depression and the uncanny knack of being able to disguise it. In fact, Mrs Imber was exceedingly obstinate. She was not going to tell her GP what the matter was if he had not picked up on it himself. Besides which, if the cause of her malaise were to be properly identified, she would be obliged to suffer having to discuss it with him.

She knew what the cause was and that no pill, no potion, could possibly cure it or even act as a palliative. Only her strong bond with Sally and their regular chats provided her with any relief. It would have helped if she had been able to share her anxieties with someone her own age, but there **was** no one. She had told herself that not even Rita would have understood what was ailing her. Nor could she contemplate burdening her daughter.

In all this, Mrs Imber might have appeared to be showing the cantankerous behaviour of an ill-tempered old woman. However, although she certainly was obstinate and impetuous, she had justification aplenty for the way that life had treated her and her husband.

Mrs Imber died on 12 August 1997.

She had no possessions other than her house in Cumbria, a dictionary, the notebook containing her Will and recipes, her wedding ring and a small silver cup the hallmarks on which were too worn to allow for any identification. There were no photos and no letters; just piles of undispensed National Health prescriptions.

4.

ALICE

It was not until Alice had reached the age of four that Mr and Mrs Bridge discovered that she could not smell smells. Whilst Sally would, from time to time, announce *"**that** smells disgusting!"* Alice, on the other hand, would not have any clue of what her sister was talking about.

When it came, the diagnosis of loss of the sense of smell, though obvious, answered many questions that had been troubling Mr and Mrs Bridge. It explained why Alice did not enjoy mealtimes or eating; why she used more salt and pepper than the other three round the table combined and possibly why she did not even like **talking** about food. However, no explanation of the cause was ever forthcoming.

Mrs Bridge was interested in the possibility that Alice's condition might also explain why her memory was not as good as Sally's. She would test their comparative ability to recall events and had found Alice wanting – although not to any serious extent. Mrs Bridge knew from her own experience that a memory which is triggered by a smell tends to be more intense. If that was correct, she thought, then it was possible that there might be a link between Alice's inability to smell effectively and her deficient memory. Six months later, Mrs Bridge went to see her GP about herself and he asked after Alice and Sally. Mrs Bridge reminded him of the absence of Alice's sense of smell, but the GP told her that the only treatment would involve an operation which no one wanted.

"No, of course not, but could there be any connection with her loss of memory?"

"That is possible," the GP replied, *"because the part of the brain which processes the senses of smell and taste sit near to those parts which deal with memory and emotion and has links to them, but we don't know very much about this. Is Alice's memory particularly wanting?"*

Mrs Bridge told her doctor that Alice's forgetfulness was not too serious and that Sally's memory was fine.

"Well, I suggest that you monitor Alice's position over the next three months and let me know if anything gets worse. Is that OK with you?"

Ultimately, the issue did not seem to worry Alice and it moved down Mr and Mrs Bridge's list of parental worries. The Bridges were more interested in how Alice and Sally, with identical genes, upbringing and schooling, were nevertheless developing distinct personalities and physical traits.

"I guess," said Mrs Bridge during a discussion between them about the girls, *"that we are all influenced differently by our environment and that it would be most improbable that their personalities would develop in parallel."*

Mr Bridge was not so sure. *"There was that story in the newspaper, though, about identical twins separated at birth. When they were eventually reunited, it turned out they had partners with the same name, owned dogs of the same breed, had an aversion to the same foods and even used the same brand of toothpaste!"*

Mrs Bridge laughed. *"I bet, nonetheless, that they had very different personalities, especially having grown up apart."*

And so it was the case that, from an early age, the personalities of Alice and Sally diverged to the point where they themselves started to recognise it. That divergence did not, however, extend to affect their mutual love for playing word games together.

"Can we play a game of 'Ghosts'?" Alice asked as the two of them sauntered back from school one bright summer afternoon.

'Ghosts' was their favourite word game. It involved one player choosing a letter of the alphabet and the other, having a particular word in mind, calling out another letter to be placed after that letter and so on. The first player to complete a word of more than three letters loses a life. If a player challenges and there is no possible word with the string of letters so far called out, then the other player loses a life.

"… let's make it 'Superghosts'," replied Sally, *"so we can also add a letter to the front. I'll begin – U."*

"N" came from Alice, followed by *"D"* from Sally, then **R** from Alice and an **E** from Sally.

"Naughty," Alice replied playfully, adding an **S** at the end and thinking of the word '**UNDRESS**'. She took it that she must have won that round because if Sally were to add another *"S"* after hers, then Sally would have completed a word and lose a life.

"I've got you there!" Alice cried, *"... what are you going to do now?"*

"Well I, too, will add another 'S' – but at the front!"

◆ ◆ ◆

It was the case that, in time, either out of laziness or a desire to use their combined resources effectively, they began to rely on each other to assume those tasks the other did not enjoy or was not as good at. If they had maths and geography homework, for example, Sally would do the maths and Alice the geography, which they would swap for the other to copy. They were able to employ this stratagem for months without alerting their parents, however, it did raise suspicion at school, for it was not difficult for their teachers to spot that they were both making the same mistakes in their homework. Their English teacher noticed first. She took them aside after school one day and came right out with it. She warned them that they would have to stop copying each other's work. The fact that neither twin denied anything confirmed Miss Creasey's suspicions, and she went on to make the point that they would not be able to *"hold hands in exams"* and *"while there was nothing wrong with helping each other out occasionally"* they would learn only if they made sure that they each tackled their homework separately. The girls were sensible enough to understand this and they promised Miss Creasey that they would not cheat again on their English homework. That response was somewhat insincere because they so much enjoyed working in co-operation with each other on school things and would find it hard to kick the habit entirely.

They had been applying a similar technique to their chores at home, where they collaborated with each other by relying on the strengths of the more accomplished twin in any particular endeavour.

There was one significant example of this. Neither Alice nor Sally appeared to communicate much with their parents on anything important in life. Perhaps the bond between the girls made this unnecessary. Perhaps their parents were unable to establish meaningful relationships with anyone other than each other; the unit consisting of Mr and

Mrs Bridge was, indeed, like that of twins. How such a situation could have arisen in the Bridge family is a matter of conjecture. The natural feelings of parents towards their children – deeply embedded maternal and paternal inclinations – had in this case failed to take root and to flourish.

But there it was and Alice and Sally coped with it. While their emotional instincts expected piles of love and affection from their parents, they were, over time, able to compensate for the lack of it because they were twins and they began to treat the absence of parental warmth and affection as the norm.

They developed techniques for coping so that, for example, it would be Alice, chiefly, who would communicate with her father while Sally was the 'liaison officer' for their mother. Alice and Sally did not plan to create such a curious arrangement – it just developed naturally.

Although this odd way of running a family might have been expected to increase the lack of cohesion in the Bridge family, it seemed, in its funny way, to help strengthen it so that the quality of Alice's relationship with their father was greater than it would have been had their father also had to worry about Sally. A corresponding arrangement subsisted between Sally and their mother.

❖ ❖ ❖

To return to Oldham Independent Grammar, the promise given to Miss Creasey was, indeed, less than genuine for the fact that the twins went on to do something much more serious than each other's homework.

Alice was to sit an end of year maths test and she knew she would get an awful mark. She could not face the prospect of bringing home a bad report, especially since her mother had spent so much time giving her extra maths coaching. Sally was in a higher set than Alice in maths and had already taken her test.

Over one whole week before the maths test, Alice embarked on an offensive to persuade Sally to take it for her. Sally laughed at first, but as the week progressed, she could see Alice becoming increasingly desperate for her to co-operate. Alice, firstly, tried to use her old trick (which Sally did not fall for this time) of insisting that since Alice was the elder of the two she deserved to be helped.

Alice then promised Sally a series of rewards. When this, too, failed, Alice used blackmail. Alice told Sally that if she did not help her out, she would tell their parents that Sally had stolen a £5 note from their mother. Although that was not true, the threat had sufficient plausibility to make Sally cave in because money had, indeed, gone missing from their mother's purse three weeks earlier; only it had not been Sally who had taken it.

In the upshot, Sally fell into the role and took Alice's maths test for her that Monday morning making sure that her appearance was as much like Alice's as possible and telling herself not to talk to anyone in Alice's set and, most importantly, not to perform too well in the test.

Halfway through the test, one of the girls sitting next to her (she did not know her name) had peered over at the calculations which Sally was busy writing down. Sally could not understand why her neighbour should be doing this since there was no one in her class who would think of cribbing from Alice Bridge's maths work. A moment later, it occurred to Sally what was really happening. The girl was not staring at Sally's answers but at the ruler on Sally's desk because it had Sally's name boldly etched onto it. On the way out of the exam room and forgetting the fact that she was not going to converse with anyone, she approached the girl:

"Hi, um, I saw you staring at the ruler … Sally gave it to me 'cos I've lost mine."

Sally relayed the whole of that story to Alice, describing the girl involved. Sally also made a point of giving her ruler to Alice for her to keep and Alice, thanked her. Sally was not sure whether that '*thank you*' was for the ruler or for her act of sisterly devotion in the face of extreme risk; she had been about to ask Alice, but Sally decided that enough had already been said and done.

When the test results were given out later that week, Alice's classmate looked quizzically at her and Alice thought for one heart-racing moment that 'the beans' were about to be spilled. However, 'Alice's' mark in the test, although decent enough, was not as high as that of her prying classmate.

And so there were no repercussions. Nothing ever came of the twins' maths duplicity – except for the realisation on Sally's part that she had been lacking excitement in her life. Nonetheless, she was not a risk-taker and told herself she would never do anything like that again and that a caper of this kind was to be roundly sat upon; not merely because it was unfair and subversive of the exam system, but because it had had the effect of making Alice feel that there was always a means by which she could get whatever she wanted; that she could 'walk on water'. Sally understood that a rounded school education should be designed to give children plenty of confidence, however, Alice was in danger of overdosing.

Whereas Sally would always 'talk through' her problems with Alice, Alice was so confident of her ability to make life's decisions on her own that she had no need to consult with anyone – least of all her parents – and would not even consult Sally except when she was faced with a homework assignment she was unable to fathom.

Alice's self-sufficiency – a quality which is of benefit to most of us – could be seen, in Alice's case, to be a handicap in that it contributed to her becoming a lonely person appearing never to need anyone else.

5.

THE BALLET

Although Alice and Sally had given up lessons a year earlier, they both continued to be enchanted by the ballet and after some polite (but constant) badgering, their parents agreed, for the girls' 14th birthday, to take them to see the Northern Ballet's Production of *The Nutcracker* at the Oldham Coliseum Theatre.

The girls and their mother talked about the anticipated trip unendingly. Their father's involvement in the planning was limited to booking four seats in the stalls and trusting that he would be able to avoid falling asleep on the night. They were expensive tickets.

A week prior to that outing, Brian, their 16-year-old next-door neighbour, had asked Alice to go ice skating with him on the very evening of the planned ballet visit. Alice had always been 'in love' with Brian. He had not previously shown any interest in Alice (nor, indeed, Sally), whilst Alice, on the other hand, was always peeking through the net curtains in the front room whenever Brian passed by.

Alice had bumped into Brian as they were each fumbling to find their front door keys on returning from school one Monday afternoon. She had been so surprised by the proposal that she had forgotten to put a smile together to go with her 'yes'. Brian was equally astounded; not only that Alice had agreed to go ice skating with him but that he had been able to muster the courage to ask her in the first place.

At supper that evening, Alice casually mentioned her encounter with Brian. There was a family discussion as to how the dilemma should be dealt with but no engagement between Sally and Alice – not even later in the privacy of their bedroom, since they were wary of any kind of confrontation.

Sally felt constrained from saying what she really thought, so strong was the monozygotic attachment. She had been looking forward to the trip to the ballet for many weeks. She had told one of her classmates about the family outing and had even decided how the four of them would sit – Pa next to Sally next to Alice next to Ma.

It was a severe blow to Sally that her identical twin, her soulmate, her confidante of 14 years, her constant companion, her best friend, her bedroom sharer, her school desk sharer, her maths test taskmaster – would contemplate being apart from her sister for even one night, let alone on their birthday. Even if Alice did, in the end, agree to go out en famille, Sally understood Alice well enough to know that she would not really mean it and that she would sulk the whole evening – and beyond.

For at least the second time in their 'career' as twins, it was clear to Sally that cracks in their togetherness were appearing – cracks which Sally had not seen coming. It had not even occurred to her, a girl of considerable intelligence, that a time would come when their lives might diverge. She felt gravely injured and so very agitated. Whenever Sally experienced emotions of this kind, she would share her state of unrest with Alice – a resource she knew was not open to her on this occasion.

But that was not the whole of it. Sally's wound was made even more painful by the pouring of a measure of jealousy into it, since she, too, had long been nurturing thoughts about Brian. Why, she conjectured, had Brian asked Alice to go out with him rather than her? They were identical twins. They dressed alike, spoke alike and she lived as close to Brian as Alice did. She could not stop punishing herself. Was she not as pretty as Alice or was there something wrong with her of which she was unaware?

Sally slowly came to understand why it was that she and Alice had never spoken together about Brian. Neither of them had even mentioned his name to the other although they had constantly exchanged giggles about intimate matters. This sudden realisation came as another blow to Sally. She persuaded herself that it was all Alice's fault, since she should immediately have told Brian she was going on a family outing that evening; and it was also Brian's fault, since he should have asked her instead of Alice but … but it was also **her** fault for not speaking to Alice about her feelings for Brian. How much stronger, she thought, would their bond have been had they talked together about their neighbour. In any event, another fault line had now appeared in their relationship whether Alice realised it or not.

For Mr and Mrs Bridge, this was one of those seminal parental dilemmas. They recognised the seriousness of the position and told the girls they would think it over and talk to them later in the week.

Mr Bridge wanted to cancel the trip, but he realised that that would give Alice the idea that she could 'pull the strings'. Mrs Bridge wanted to go ahead without Alice and, if they could, sell her ticket.

She also wondered whether Brian might want to go with them to the ballet or, alternatively, be willing to change the date but decided that involving Brian would potentially create even more stress.

As the girls' birthday approached, there was one more discussion at the supper table and it had an unexpected outcome. It was apparent from the girls' expressions and the tone of their voices that they were merely being polite and trying to avoid confrontation.

Alice was still wondering what she should do. One forlorn hope was that by being magnanimous to Sally she might suggest changing the date of the theatre visit. But Alice did not want to seem an ungrateful daughter or a disloyal sister by choosing Brian over the ballet.

"I don't really care what I do" … *"I wouldn't go ice skating unless Sally was happy for me to go."*

In truth, Alice was initially beyond eager to accept the invitation from Brian because it would, after all, be her first date.

However, on reflection, Alice began to get cold feet. She had never been ice skating and she would have no idea what to do. Even more importantly, by accepting Brian's invitation she knew she would be letting Sally down very badly. And so that was that. She told her family she did not mind missing her date with Brian and that she **would** go to the ballet.

In the upshot, no one enjoyed the girls' birthday treat; Sally and Alice both sulked; Mr Bridge fell asleep within ten valiant minutes of the overture starting; and Mrs Bridge could not concentrate – so upset was she at the tension which she could see between the girls. Brian never asked Alice out again, and most significantly the rock-solid relationship between the sisters had been uncompromisingly fractured because of that simple 'yes' Alice had given to Brian. The twin edifice called *'Sally/Alice'* had been damaged. If the girls did not understand that, their next birthday would confirm it.

Furthermore, their parents could see how the last week had sown seeds of difference and division between the two girls, who as identical twins with identical genes were possibly growing so far apart from each other that they would come to be twins only in appearance.

6.

BIRTH CERTIFICATES

It was not until Sally had reached the age of 15, exactly a year after the Oldham Coliseum outing debacle, that she realised she did not exist.

That stark realisation had come as another severe blow to the equilibrium and contentment which had accompanied her life's journey right up to her 14th birthday.

It was on the Saturday before her 15th birthday that her mother just came out with it at the breakfast table. There was no gentle lead up to it. There was no warning. Instead of a *'did you sleep well?'* or a *'do you want your usual breakfast'*, it was:

"Sally, I am afraid you cannot go to France in August with the school."

It took a while before Sally could fully understand what her mother was talking about. Habit had conditioned her to expect something much more mundane at the kitchen table on a Saturday morning.

"What did you say?"

"I am afraid you won't be going to Quimper."

"What!? … Will Alice and I be going elsewhere or are we all going away together somewhere else?"

"No, Sally, it's not that."

Mrs Bridge was looking sheepish.

"Then what on earth is it? Does Alice know?"

Alice was still in bed.

"It's complicated."

"What does that mean?"

Sally was angry and confused.

"I have just heard from the Passport Office that they won't give you a passport."

"Why on earth not? Was the application form filled out wrongly?"

"No, that's not what it is."

"Well, what is it then?"

"There is something wrong with your birth certificate."

"And also Alice's?"

Sally had begun to suspect that Alice did not have the same problem; otherwise she would not still be in bed.

"No. Alice already has her passport. It's just yours which is the problem."

"Why's that?"

At this point, Mr Bridge sloped into the kitchen having all the bearing of a relief brigade coming to the rescue. He must have been listening outside the kitchen door which grated with Sally, since she did not approve of any kind of spying. He stood behind Sally, rested his hands on his head, fingers entwined and began to explain things to her she had never previously been aware of.

It transpired that when Mrs Bridge was seven months' pregnant they had gone to Turkey for a two-week holiday. Towards the end of their stay, Mrs Bridge was taken into hospital by way of an emergency. She was ready to give birth to the twins and she was agitated that Mr Bridge had gone off to get some shopping that afternoon, leaving her essentially alone in a foreign country at such a crucial time.

Immediately after the births, her parents, eager to leave Turkey on the first available flight, had, en route to the airport, grabbed the emergency travel documents from the hospital and the four of them had only just caught their flight home. Their parents had taken it that those papers included two valid birth certificates.

Sally could tell from this that her parents had some further bad news for her and she waited quietly in fearful anticipation.

Both Mr and Mrs Bridge continued to explain things to her; that Alice and Sally had both been issued with NHS and National Insurance numbers without any difficulty and they had no reason to assume there would be a problem with obtaining UK passports for the girls.

Sally was trying not to cry.

It seems there was some kind of problem with Sally's birth certificate, meaning it could not be accepted as a valid document. Apparently the Passport Office was extremely strict on such matters and could see no way of resolving the issue other than by the Bridges applying for Turkish nationality for Sally.

The Bridges had not previously told the girls of the problems they had encountered with the Passport Office because they had fully expected to overcome them.

It was clear to Sally that the trip to Quimper was off, but she put on a brave face.

"Alice and I could instead go down to Swansea to visit your cousins."

Sally did not begin her uncontrollable, inconsolable torrent of tears until the point at which her father told her that it would not be fair to hold Alice back from going on the Quimper trip and that it had been decided that Alice should go without her. At the mention of the word 'without', Sally felt unable to control herself any longer. It was no wonder, she thought, that Alice had remained in bed.

It took Sally the whole of the weekend to take in all that her parents had explained to her.

She was being denied her first trip abroad – and to France, when French was her favourite subject. That was more than unfair. She felt she had done nothing wrong, so why should she suffer?

Alice was to be spared; she was exempt from this 'punishment' and Sally expected she would be smug having avoided the nightmare that had just befallen her sister. Sally would not be prepared to go to Wales on her own. She had never met her Swansea cousins and was not about to do so without the support of Alice.

Sally could not believe that Alice had been so disloyal and had not even come down on that Saturday morning to give her support when she would have known what was going to unfold.

There was no real apology from her parents, no show of regret, although Sally was not certain whether this was a fair criticism; she would think about it. She **was**, however, happy to criticise her mother for being uncharacteristically harsh and unloving towards her particularly in the manner that she had broken the news. She wondered what was going on. She could not believe that such misfortune could have befallen her – but nor did she have any notion of the severity of the challenges that lay ahead as a result of her defective birth certificate and the pain she was still to suffer in consequence of it.

On the Monday after school, Alice and Sally were to go out together to celebrate their birthday.

Although Sally was hardly in the mood the two of them did go off to a bakery in Oldham called *Bakes and Cakes*, where they could indulge and chat.

"I'm sorry I didn't come downstairs on Saturday ... it's just, um, Ma said it would only make things more difficult for you ... she's under a lot of stress, you know ... I don't know why. But it might explain why she was so brusque with you, Sally."

Alice was very sisterly and very apologetic to Sally over the fact that she was not also going to Quimper. *"Y'know it's all paid for, and I guess it's better for Ma and Pa that they don't lose money for **both** of our trips ... that would be silly."* In Sally's eyes, that was not nearly sufficient reason for her being left at home, but she dropped all further discussion on the subject. It was, after all, their birthday treat and Alice had offered to pay..

"Look, Sally, I feel really bad ... but I promise I'll do what I can to help."

As Alice took out her purse from her school jacket, her passport fell to the floor. Sally picked it up and, looking at it longingly, handed it to Alice.

" Alice, please explain to me just why you are you carrying this around with you? What would happen if you lost it?"

"I don't know. Perhaps it would be sensible if I got a photocopy for you to look after … just in case."

They immediately went next door to the newsagents and took a copy.

In Sally's mind, Alice was a warrior.

She was fearless, adventurous and impetuous. She acted first and thought about the consequences later. She acted only for the moment so that investing for the long term never appealed to her. That is why studying and school itself was of little importance to Alice and why, for her, time spent on forging friendships was a waste of time. Sally knew that her sister did love her, but she was not certain how dependable their relationship was likely to be.

If Alice was a warrior, then Sally was a worrier.

She would think carefully about everything that she was proposing to do and then analyse it when she had done it. She was always careful, meticulous and studious and would not take risks. She loved Alice deeply and understood her, although she did not understand how identical twins, so close in their attachment to each other, could be so different in temperament, and more pressingly she did not understand how Alice could even think of going off to Quimper without her.

Perhaps out of a feeling of guilt Alice had on several occasions volunteered to discuss the problem of Sally's defective Turkish birth certificate with her in order to help Sally feel less anxious. But that was a difficult task, since the issue (which Sally had come to call the *'BC problem'*) was constantly playing on her mind, as was the school trip she was about to miss.

Come August, Alice and her passport, all clean and gleaming, departed in somewhat of a rush from home at 5:30am to get to the front gates of Oldham Independent Grammar School in time to catch the coach which would take nearly the whole class via the Channel to Quimper. Sally's absence from the trip was a surprise to most of the class; Alice merely shrugged her shoulders when asked the reason for it.

Sally herself was also learning to shrug **her** shoulders despite her misfortune. She told herself that she must not let the *BC problem* play on her mind, at least for the next year or so; she did not want to be distracted from her GCSEs.

7.
PARENTS' NAMES

Alice and Sally did not know their parents' first names – not even their initials.

By resolutely withholding this information from their children, Mr and Mrs Bridge were depriving them of their family story. It was as if their parents were criminals seeking to hide their identities.

Alice and Sally, of course, knew (or, at least, they thought they knew) their parents' surname – and therefore their own. They were also aware of the pet names their parents called each other – mother calling their father *'Georgie'* and father calling their mother *'Porgie'*. This much their parents had revealed. But they knew no more.

When Sally was 10 years old she had asked her mother on the bus coming home from the shops what her mother's real first name was. The unexpected fierceness of the response (which Sally relayed to Alice that evening) seemed to Sally to fill the whole bus and it so embarrassed her that neither she nor Alice sought to investigate further the given names of either parent again. The issue had ceased to be relevant to them and it did not occur to them to explore further or seek to solve the mystery, because, for the girls, there **was** no mystery. Alice and Sally came to accept their parents' strange behaviour as the norm.

Neither Mr nor Mrs Bridge owned a computer or cell phone. They had installed two separate letterboxes outside their front door, one for themselves and one for the girls; and the postman had learnt to co-operate.

More significantly, Mr and Mrs Bridge had no friends. Sadly, they did not even class their children as friends, since in the imperative to hide themselves away, their children were the opposition. The Bridges did not belong to any clubs or groups. It is a horrible word, but it must be used – they were 'loners'.

There was one particular respect in which the charade of camouflaging their names played out, and it is possibly the most significant. The house rules, enforced rigidly by Mr and Mrs Bridge, included a ban on the girls entering their parents' bedroom at any time, which to Alice and Sally felt like a form of psychological abuse, since there never existed an opportunity for Ma to usher a distraught Alice or a frightened Sally into her bed to comfort them and repair whatever hurt they might be suffering at the time. For the girls never to be able to share the warmth, the intimacy of the parental bed in such circumstances was yet another squandered opportunity to strengthen family ties. Whether or not their parents' bedroom was being used, the door was always locked.

Mrs Bridge 'did not do' affection, and although Mr Bridge was an attentive father, it would be inaccurate to say that he was a **loving** father. He always sought to avoid physical contact with the girls – and they never saw him display any token of affection towards their mother.

Whereas most parents are instinctively (perhaps genetically) drawn to hold, hug and harbour their children, whatever their age, the Bridges pushed their daughters away. Mr and Mrs Bridge's bedroom, had it not been out of bounds to Alice and Sally, would have revealed the books their parents were reading, the post they received, the photos and pictures they chose for the walls and also their names. There was so much secrecy that there remained little room for love. Deprived of water, plants wither. Being deprived of the opportunity to engage with their parents, Alice and Sally suffered.

And there was yet something else that Alice and Sally were unaware of, namely, that Mr and Mrs Bridge had a visceral fear of religion and an urge to protect their children from it.

Most absurd, thought the girls, was their parents' hatred of all things German, to the point where Mr Bridge even feared the umlaut – the two dots used on some vowels in German and in a few other languages. This strange phobia – exemplified by Mr Bridge's change of name from 'Brücke' to 'Bridge' – had, furthermore, rubbed off on Mrs Bridge.

All this was difficult for the girls to understand. They had heard their father rant about the umlaut on so many occasions that they had devised their own private codeword for his behaviour – they dubbed it 'FOU' – *fear of umlauts*.

"I've looked it up. It's called 'onomatophobia'," said Sally to Alice after yet another outburst from their father one evening, *"... the fear of certain words or names, which can, apparently, be brought on by someone having a traumatic experience which they associate with a particular word."*

For the girls, this definition may have explained the meaning of *'onomatophobia'*, but it did not help to clarify why their parents were bringing them up in such a bizarre fashion. The definition only served to deepen the mystery.

Bit by bit, Alice and Sally were realising that they were being denied a normal upbringing and they wondered what that might mean for the future.

8.
SALLY

Sally was pleased to go back to school after the summer holidays. She had done well in her GCSEs if not as well as her teachers had predicted.

Alice's results, on the other hand, were not particularly good and, for her, the prospect of returning to school was unthinkable since she knew that there was now a measure against which she would always be judged. Alice did not begrudge Sally her grades nor was she fussed with her own results. She had achieved five GCSEs and that would be a sufficient academic achievement to send her on her life's journey. Alice was, in fact, quite satisfied with her results because, had she done better, it would have been much more difficult for her to resist parental and school pressure to continue her education. She had never been prepared to devote that much effort to school; the thought of leaving and being able to travel was much more appealing. Alice felt exhilarated by her life-changing decision not to proceed with her schooling – all the more so having taken it without discussing it with her parents, Sally or any of her teachers.

When Sally walked into her classroom on the first morning back, she breathed in the freshness, anticipation and excitement of seeing faces she had not seen for six weeks. She felt that such a heady atmosphere was to be treasured, since it might not last – and, indeed, it didn't. Alice's absence weighed heavy on her and brought back lots of unpleasant thoughts. Sally was upset that, for the first time, she was at school without her twin sister. She was also upset about Alice's results. For Sally, the magic of the first day of term had ended in its opening minute.

To the question *'Where's Alice?'*, Sally replied, without artifice, by means of a simple shrug of the shoulders, echoing Alice's shrug the previous month on the bus to Quimper.

If Alice's shrug on that bus had meant *'I don't care'*, Sally's meant *'I don't know'*. In fact, no one knew where Alice was. She had gone backpacking on her own without saying where. She did not even say when she might be returning. The last postcard home from her had been sent two months ago from Cartagena in Spain. It had been addressed to Sally and simply bore the quickly scribbled message: *'Weather is here. Wish you were beautiful'*.

Sally had never had any experience of how to make friends but now that her sister was not around, she would have to try.

She did not have to try too hard because several of the girls who had previously wanted to make friends with her, but had been put off by the twins' closeness, now seemed chattier. Sally was shy, but when she got going, she was easy to talk to and entertaining. She was able to make friends with two girls in her class whom she had hardly spoken to before – Rhianne and Freya. Sally was so pleased that neither the natural cliquishness of her class nor the geekishness of her interests had discouraged the possibility of new friendships. They talked about their holidays, their taste in music, the boys at the boys' school they had spoken to on the way to school, getting a job in the Christmas holidays and, into the bargain, some of Sally's hobbies.

Sally told the girls that she liked learning about words and their origins and that she always carried a dictionary with her. That would have been enough to put a distance between Sally and most of her classmates, but Rhianne and Freya appeared to be interested. Maybe they were merely being polite.

"What do you mean," asked Rhianne, *"give me an example."*

"Well, I can give you two if you want. Did you know that the word 'clue' comes from 'clew' C – L – E – W, which is an old word meaning a ball of string like the one Theseus used to help him get out of the labyrinth? And 'matrix', which we did yesterday with Mrs Barnes in maths, comes from mater, which is Latin for mother and -ix, indicating the womb, which enables things to be generated."

This resulted in a few nervous laughs from both Rhianne and Freya before they moved on to another topic of conversation.

Despite the fact that Rhianne and Freya seemed to have different interests from her, merely thinking about her two new friends was an effective way of taking Sally's mind off other things – in particular, the *'BC problem'*. But it was not too long before Sally found herself again dwelling on her concerns and writing them out on the bus home from school. The list of concerns was lengthy and the longer it got, the shorter her fingernails:

- **Won't be able to get a passport**

- **... so can't go abroad**

- **What about an identity card?**

- **Can I open a bank account?**

- **Will I be able to get a part-time job?**

- **Can I get a credit card?**

- **Will I be able to apply to uni?**

- **Can I get a student loan?**

- **What about getting into a pub?**

Sally suspected that there were many other things which might affect her as she got older, such as getting married, applying for a mortgage, getting a driving licence and voting in elections. She felt overwhelmed, particularly because she had only her mother to talk to.

However, her mother was consoling and sensible. They had never chatted for so long together. Now that Alice was not at home, things were possibly different.

"Sweetheart, for the moment, this isn't going to impact on your life."

"Sweetheart, for the moment, this isn't going to impact on your life."

"What about the school trip I've missed?"

"Yes, but I promise I will try to put this right. Let's start immediately by writing a letter to the Passport Office. Who knows? Perhaps they will change their mind."

She was temporarily placated by the promise of action and the letter to the Passport Office which her mother wrote and posted that evening. As a result Sally went to bed more content than she had been for some time.

The next morning, she took the BC list with her to school and decided that, at the present time, the most important and pressing item on the list was whether she could get a job during the holidays. Her friends would be applying soon and she did not want to miss out.

After school that day she went into Dukinfield Library to use their computers; she wanted to know more about the process of applying for a part-time job but ended up learning more from Doris, one of the librarians. *"You'll have to prove who you are … that you have the right to work in the UK … and show a passport, or birth certificate."*

Although she had been expecting that response it nevertheless came as a blow; she wished that Alice was on hand to help her. Maybe that was the reason for the dream Sally had that night in which Alice appeared on stage in South America.

The following afternoon on the way home from school, Sally went into Hempels Supermarket (one of three branches in Greater Manchester) where she asked to see the assistant manager in charge of recruiting part-timers. The process was unexpectedly brief. A young man, who looked no more than a couple of years older than Sally, saw her within half an hour and asked her some questions. He told her that there were a few vacancies for Christmas if she acted quickly; and Sally did. She completed an Application Form page 2 of which confirmed the need for her passport. She took out from her bag the photocopy of Alice's passport which she handed to the assistant manager.

"Will this do?"

He looked at it, then looked at Sally and saw that Sally was, indeed, Alice.

"Thanks. That'll be fine."

And so it came to pass that on one and the same day 'Alice Bridge' became a shelf-filler at Hempels in Oldham, a hitchhiker in Murcia and an actress in Sao Paulo.

Sally really enjoyed her temporary part-time holiday job in Hempels as a customer assistant or shelf-filler, known as a 'WSH' – a 'Weekly Shelf Handler'. Time seemed to pass quickly and the people around her were very friendly and supportive.

Outside of work, things were stressful. Sally could hardly talk about a job she had taken under her sister's name, and she had to deny to her friends that she even **had** a part-time job. That made it difficult for Sally to forge close relationships – particularly because getting a holiday job was one of the hottest topics of discussion.

She was also under some stress at work because of her concern that one of her school friends might come into the store, recognise Sally and say something which would reveal that she was not Alice. Indeed, taking up the supermarket job again during half term, Sally's luck nearly ran out. She was pushing a trolley full of boxes of diet coke down the soft drinks aisle when she saw Rhianne coming towards her. There was nowhere for Sally to hide.

"Hi, wow, you're working here ... how come?"

"Oh, er, hi Rhianne, look, I can't actually talk right now but promise I'll phone you later."

"That's fine. Thanks, Sally," Rhianne shouted, with a flamboyant goodbye wave.

It was no more than half an hour later that Sally's line manager asked her to redo some display labels.

" ... and Alice, by the way, how come your friend just now called you Sally?"

"Oh ... you must have misheard her. She said 'Thanks, Allie', which is what she always calls me."

,

9.

CATCH-22

Sally had been looking ahead to university and had applied to the London School of Economics to study law. She would be able to get a place there if she obtained three A* A-levels.

And she did just that.

Only one other girl in Sally's year performed better and Sally received praise and compliments from her school, her friends and from her parents. Alice, now back in England and living in Leeds with someone she had met on her travels, was more thrilled for Sally than anyone else and sent her a leather shoulder bag by way of congratulations.

The achievement – a giant leap forward in Sally's continuing education – was marred by the fact that, in the eyes of the Student Loans Company, she did not exist; at least Sally could not prove her identity to their satisfaction or, indeed, to the satisfaction of anybody. No doubt, she thought, LSE would also require the same proof.

This bizarre situation was now beginning to threaten Sally's prospects.

Sally regretted not having started to tackle the BC problem much earlier and that she had allowed herself to think she could get by with Alice's photocopied passport. She realised that this had lulled her into a false sense of well-being and she determined to resolve the problem once and for all. The one person she thought could help her was Alice, even if their relationship was now more distant.

Sally decided to invite herself up to Leeds for the weekend.

Alice was delighted that her younger sister wanted to visit and told her that although she had only a small bedsit, Sally could sleep very comfortably on the sofa. Alice and Sally would have plenty of time to chat together alone, since Jose (whom Alice had met on her travels in Spain) would be out with friends on the Friday evening.

Upon Sally's arrival that evening, Alice went wild congratulating her on her A-levels results and her place at LSE and then embarked on a long discourse about her extensive tour of Spain and how she had met Jose. She liked him a lot but theirs, she volunteered, was nothing like a permanent relationship; merely one of mutual convenience.

"Hitch-hiking is so much safer as a couple ... and it helped that Jose is Spanish ... and you know, it was so much cheaper travelling as a pair."

"Is he good-looking?"

"Oh yes! You'll see for yourself – but, to be honest, I'm relieved he's going back to Spain. I just get bored with his company. Actually he's going back to Barcelona next week to finish his degree in Data Science. I don't think I am going to miss him but I won't know until he has gone."

Sally laughed and then suddenly felt sad; she couldn't believe that it had been two years since she had seen Alice. They had a lot of catching up to do.

When it came to Sally's turn, she well knew that her tales of Oldham would not be nearly as glamorous as Alice's account of her experiences in Spain and she kept them short; anyway, she had more important things to discuss with Alice and before she could think it through, she found herself blurting out the fact that she had used Alice's identity to get a job in Hempels.

"Alice, I am so embarrassed that I actually did that!"

There was long pause and then a burst of laughter from Alice.

"You didn't think I would mind, did you? I'm delighted … I had been wondering what I could do to fill out my CV!"

Sally was relieved and they bonded in a prolonged bout of laughter, which was followed, seconds later, by more laughter.

Sally felt it was the right time to broach the subject of her place at LSE and getting a student loan.

"The list of occasions on which I will need to prove that I'm 'Sally Bridge' goes on and on. This is all so awfully stressful. I want to be me again whoever 'me' is! I've worked so hard to get to uni and just as I get past the final hurdle, this effing obstacle has stopped me dead."

Sally suddenly found herself in tears.

"Sally, I think I can understand how you feel. I've been thinking of you a lot … It seems to me that the best way to deal with the problem is for me to go to Turkey

and try to sort it out for you. I can't promise anything at all, but if I could find someone in authority there, I might be able to get your birth certificate corrected or a new one issued or something."

"You'd really be prepared to do that, Alice?"

"Of course. I'd really like to help sort this out for you. To be truthful, I've been looking for the next place to go on my travels and Turkey will do as well as anywhere else. Did you know that Turkey is a great jumping off place for some exotic countries? I have always fancied going to Kazakhstan."

Sally beamed and gave Alice a prolonged hug; it was so comforting to be a twin. She doubted whether any other variety of sibling would have been anywhere near as prepared to take on a task of this kind. Although Alice had no need of help from Sally, she also realised the strength of their attachment and so a kind of closeness was beginning to return to the twins.

That evening they began to make some plans. They talked about how Sally might contribute towards the trip to Turkey; about her speaking to UCAS and also to the LSE Admissions office regarding the possibility of deferring her place while all this was going on. There a lot to discuss.

Despite the lateness of the hour, Alice went on to tell Sally more stories of her travels in Spain to which Sally, relieved to have time out from her troubles, listened in enrapt silence – that is until Jose returned home. Neither in his presence nor personality was he very different from the image of him that Sally had been building up in her mind. He was, indeed, very good-looking. He was dark-haired, clean-shaven, stylishly dressed and very easy to talk to. Within an hour of his arrival, Sally was learning things about Alice of which even she had not been aware and which she was unlikely to have learned merely from chatting to Alice – that, for example, she had read the whole of the works of Stefan Zweig, was scared of being accidentally buried underground and that she had recently taken up playing chess with Jose.

❖ ❖ ❖

In the week following Sally's return to Ashton-under-Lyne, she talked to Alice constantly on the phone. Alice's mission would not be an easy one to accomplish since there was at least one formidable Catch-22 in their path. If Alice was to help Sally obtain a new Turkish birth certificate to enable her to prove her identity, Sally would have to grant

Alice a valid Power of Attorney authorising her to act on her behalf. However, before Sally could create any such Power of Attorney, she would need to prove her identity.

And as they talked they realised there was another Catch-22. If Alice was **not** able to help Sally obtain a new Turkish birth certificate then Sally would have to travel to Turkey to sort things out, but without a passport she could not leave the country.

Sally could see no solution to this conundrum; to this seemingly never-ending Kafkaesque nightmare of mindless bureaucracy. It seemed to her that she was being punished even though she had done nothing wrong.

The girls decided that the only possible way forward would be to attend the Turkish Consulate Office in London. They made an appointment for the following week to meet Emre who seemed on the telephone to be sympathetic.

Most of their three-hour meeting with him concerned how it might be possible for a Power of Attorney granted by Sally to be notarially certified according to Turkish law despite the fact that Sally had no passport.

Emre promised he would do his best to help. He kept flitting in and out of their meeting room to seek guidance from his superiors, and on each occasion he disappeared (sometimes for as much as half an hour) Sally and Alice were left in nervous anticipation – that is until Emre appeared with a large smile on his face and a sign-off from his immediate superior. Emre told them the Consulate was prepared *'on this occasion'* to accept that, for the purposes of Turkish notarisation, Sally's birth certificate should be treated as proof of the fact that she did really exist!

Sally and Alice were impressed with Emre's determination and co-operation and thought it a pity that he did not also have the authority to correct defective Turkish birth certificates.

Once Alice had gathered the information she needed for her forthcoming trip, they travelled from Kings Cross back to Manchester where Sally kept Alice company until she had boarded her connection to Leeds.

Two days later, Sally took another crucial step forward. After she had explained her predicament to LSE's Undergraduate Admissions office, they agreed to defer her place for a year – or, if she needed it, for two.

10.
PATIENCE

Alice went off to Turkey three weeks later and Sally began to have cause for hope.

However, she knew she would have to be patient. Alice told her that she would start the process of talking to the Turkish authorities only after she had done some thorough groundwork and had a good idea of how the system worked. Sally agreed that such an approach was sensible; in any event, she would have to rely completely on Alice since there was no one else who could do what she was doing for Sally.

Sally was well aware that Alice was not good at keeping in touch and, as it turned out, it was nearly a fortnight before Sally got her first update. Had

Sally been paying someone to take on this difficult (and sensitive) assignment for her then she might have had cause for complaint.

In the meantime, a three-starred A-level student called 'Sally', but who goes by the name of 'Alice', returned to stack shelves in Hempels.

Hempels had by then been taken over by the Lidburys chain and Sally was offered a promotion that involved working at a larger branch. She turned down the offer for fear she might be asked to provide fresh proof of her identity. Sally could not take the chance. In any event, it would have involved a change of bus and only 20p more per hour. It was an easy decision for Sally to make.

It was a whole six months before Alice was able to report any real progress. In April, she emailed Sally about a meeting with a senior Turkish official who thought he might be able to offer some assistance, given his cousin had been in a similar position some years back. Alice went on to say, however, that the official did not speak good English and that she was not confident that they were 'on the same page'.

She also told Sally that she was ready to seek help from a Turkish lawyer if need be, but that would involve unknown fees and possibly interfere with the informal approach that she had so far adopted and which she believed was likely to be more likely to bear fruit.

Sally was dismayed to learn a few weeks later that Alice was dating the official since she thought this might compromise Alice's efforts. Once again, Sally's expectations took another dip. She could not see how she would, at this rate, be able to get to LSE in September.

Then, suddenly, a few days after Alice had announced her 'relationship', she telephoned Sally to say that '*they*' had now looked into the details of Sally's birth certificate and would be issuing an amended one within a fortnight. They had found what they thought was the likely problem and that this could, they anticipated, be corrected. Apparently, by comparing Sally's birth certificate with Alice's, they had found that, instead of the hospital filling in the **date** of Sally's birth on her birth certificate, they had inserted the **time** of her birth.

The quality of the phoneline was not good, but Sally was in no doubt that she had heard Alice correctly and yet it took several moments for Alice's words to sink in. This was the first positive news she had received in a long time. For Sally it was like finally being told that she had been cured of a long and severely protracted illness.

◆ ◆ ◆

Sally received the couriered package three days later and wasted no time in sending the documents to the Passport Office along with an application form for her first passport. She was confident that everything was in order and excited that she would soon be in a position to call LSE to confirm her start in September. For the first time she would be able, with the help of a shining new passport, to prove who she was and that she **did** now exist. Not only that, she felt she would now be entitled to take pride in the fact that she was also a citizen of the European Union.

During a long and effusive phone call, Sally thanked Alice for the huge sacrifice she had made over the past eighteen months.

"Don't be so silly! It wasn't a sacrifice – and I've found myself a man ... will tell you about it soon. Got to go. Luv ya!"

Sally's thoughts came to rest on what she could do to thank Alice. She told herself that no gift, no gesture would be too great a thank you.

11.
LSE

Sally had to make hurried arrangements for both a student loan and her student accommodation. She had also been given a large amount of reading matter to get through before the start of term. She could so easily have missed out had Alice not sorted things in Turkey, and she would not squander this opportunity or hold back from seeking a good degree.

She did work hard that first academic year and came near the top of her class in three of the courses she had to cover.

Although Sally still found it hard to establish friendships she found a kindred spirit in Doreen Okanwe who had the same studious approach to studying. They kept each other on track in getting through the prodigious amount of work with which they were confronted and encouraged each other to minimise disruption to the daily timetable of work they set for themselves. They always sat next to each other in lectures and in the Law Library where, whenever they had been given a long list of cases to read, they would make the best use of their time by sharing the task of locating the appropriate law reports. They also went halves on course books.

By the second year, fellow students had begun to notice their diligent (if not over-zealous) approach to study.

Sally did not exclude herself, however, from all there was on offer outside the Law Library and went to almost all of the LSE Film Society's screenings and most of the lectures put on by the History Society. She took *Krav Maga* lessons (designed specially to help women learn self-defence techniques) and participated in a number of ad hoc courses intended to help students learn skills such as speed-reading and how to develop better listening skills.

It was in joining the Labour Society that Sally met someone. It was after a lecture by Lord Myners on the banking system and the overpayment of senior bank executives in February 2009 that the man sitting directly behind Sally tapped her gently on the shoulder.

"Hi, I'm Alan Field. Can I introduce myself?"

Well, he had already done so!

He didn't seem to be a typical student; he was wearing a suit and was far too polished in his mannerisms.

"Can I buy you a coffee upstairs? I won't keep you long."

It was late and she wanted to get home. However, there was something in his voice – in particular in its timbre – which she found mildly attractive. She was intrigued; particularly since she was certain that Alan Field was not a fellow student.

She hesitated; she was in no mood that evening to be sociable, particularly with a stranger. However, acting on impulse (a characteristic which ordinarily was alien to Sally) she simply nodded, and they left the lecture hall together.

It was not surprising that Sally had attracted the attention of Alan Field. Sally was 5ft 7in tall with shoulder-length brunette hair, dark brown eyes, a beautiful symmetrical face, a well-proportioned, curvaceous body and a delightful Mancunian accent. However, it was not her body that had attracted Alan Field.

Alan Field returned to their table with two coffees and a plate of chocolate biscuits and proceeded to explain to Sally that what he needed to tell her was to be kept confidential. Sally did not respond but waited nervously for what was to come next. He did not beat about the bush.

"What I would like to know, quite simply, is whether you might be prepared to consider working for the country … in our intelligence services."

Sally started to laugh.

"Is this a wind- up?" And with that she got up to leave.

"Sally, please stay. I don't want to alarm you, but the fact is we know quite a lot about you … we think that you are very talented and would fit in with the team well. You would obviously want to know much more before you might agree to anything and you would, of course, be free to back out at any time."

Alan Field paused. Sally didn't know what to say or whether she could trust him and she remained silent.

"I know that this must seem like an ambush … it is to everyone I approach. Please accept my apology for

contacting you in this way but I hope you will appreciate that there is no easy way to initiate a dialogue such as this."

Sally questioned the term *'dialogue'* since, so far, Sally had nodded once and uttered not a word. She persisted in saying nothing and Alan Field looked around the empty tables to make sure no one was in earshot.

"If you ask me to, I will get up and go … never darken your doorstep again!" he added with a touch of whimsy.

Sally dismissed this with a wave of her hand.

"Are you MI5 or MI6?"

"I am sorry, but I can't tell you any more at this stage."

"You do know that I am only a student … just a second-year student?"

"We do know that, yes."

Sally looked at Alan Field and began to feel sorry for him; he had to be at a low level in the intelligence services, she thought, otherwise he would be out hunting spies and decoding secret messages.

She looked down and reminded herself of her promise to concentrate on her law degree … yet her life had always been so unexciting…

"Can I think about it?"

"By all means, Sally. I'll be back in a week; meet me here, midday."

As Alan Field got into the lift, he raised his hand slightly in a goodbye. Sally doubled back to the café and asked the girl behind the counter whether she had ever seen the man she had just left with, but she wasn't sure.

Although the following morning she was bursting to tell Doreen about her encounter, Sally mentioned nothing; she was proud of her discretion and her ability to keep a secret.

A week later, Sally arrived early and sat at the same table. She had not needed a week to make up her mind.

" Welcome onboard Sally … you're going to be a great agent."

He shook her hand vigorously. Sally was quite excited by all this.

"Will you be my handler?" she blurted out, without thinking.

Alan looked her straight in the eyes. She felt herself blushing and was immediately angry with herself.

"It's possible, Sally, but for now you need to carry on the law degree and don't worry if it's a while before you hear from me again."

It was quite an anti-climax for Sally, but at least she could get back to her essay on *"What are the essential differences between suing for damages in negligence as opposed to in tort?"*

Sally did not hear from Alan Field for the rest of that year and she began to feel she never would again.

Her daydreams of engaging in a twilight existence travelling around the world on exciting Mata Hari-like life-and-death missions for the benefit of her country began to fade, although she could not completely give up on the possibility that her tedious existence might yet be invigorated.

Sally contemplated telling Alice about her meetings with Alan Field, not out of a desire to gossip but to make sense of them. However, she starved that temptation of any oxygen – not so much out of duty to keep the confidence but more because she wanted to keep the intrigue for her own consumption.

One particular thought bothered Sally; it was that if she **did** get some kind of post in the intelligence services, she would, yet again, be constrained from speaking to others about her job. That had been a difficult enough challenge for her working at Hempels but would be a much tougher one in a job subject to the Official Secrets Act.

Thoughts of this kind kept recurring to her over the next few months but she came to dismiss each of them as soon as they came into her head. She told herself that the 'tap on the shoulder' was most likely a hoax of some sort. What possible use would a law student be in intelligence? What purpose would a girl from Oldham serve whose life experience had consisted of filling shelves in a supermarket? Perhaps they had taken all that into consideration. Or could all this be connected with her BC problem? What if they thought she was Alice? It was all so uncertain and she felt the need to talk to Alice more than ever.

Sally realised that it would not be easy to eradicate all the high-flown notions that had now taken root. However, as time passed she was able to demote her two meetings with Alan Field from the status of *'exciting adventures'* to *'pointless encounters'* and to restrict her thinking of them only to the occasions she might need a short nap in the Law Library to overcome the tedium of ploughing through *The All England Law Reports*.

12.
GRANDMA AND SALLY

Mr and Mrs Bridge knew that when Sally came to learn of Alice's inheritance in their grandmother's Will she would feel justifiably aggrieved. That is why they put off telling her; they hoped they would never have to.

It was, in fact, Alice who told Sally about the gift by way of a small message on a twenty-first birthday card which Sally had nearly missed. There were just a few words scribbled on the back of the card telling Sally that Alice had received notification of her inheritance of the house in Lowca. Those few words were merely accompanied by three large exclamation marks.

When Sally read this she did, indeed, feel badly wronged. She felt that her birthdays always seemed to bring bad news. She was utterly taken aback that her grandmother, whom she had loved dearly, would have favoured Alice over her; Alice who had shown their grandmother little attention or affection. Sally immediately got on the phone to her mother who explained that the Will was made well before Sally's birth and could not possibly have been intended to show any preference towards Alice.

"I can't accept that – grandma could have changed her Will once we were born. There was plenty of time for her to do so before she died."

Whilst Sally's response was correct, it did not take into account the fact that once her grandmother's Will had been signed and witnessed it had been put away, both in her hideaway and in her mind, so that the significance and contents of her Will would have long been forgotten by her.

"Why couldn't you have stopped her, Ma … you knew what she was going to put in her Will."

Mrs Bridge explained on the phone how she had been too preoccupied with her pregnancy at the time to have really thought about it.

"In any event, Sally, you know your grandma was obstinate ... she just wanted the first born to have it ..."

*"We were born only **minutes** apart Ma!!"*

Sally was angry. Even allowing for her mother's pre-occupation with other things at the time, her mother could have arranged for the Will to be rewritten – something Sally had read was legally possible if done within two years after a death. Sally's mother was the Executor. Her mother could have tried to get Alice to agree to alter the Will to ensure that their grandmother's house would go to Alice and Sally equally. That, thought Sally, would have been the only proper thing to do.

Maybe Sally's mother had tried to do that, but it was now far too late. On hanging up the phone it crossed Sally's mind that her mother might possibly have decided to compensate her by leaving more to her in her own Will than to Alice, but she immediately felt ashamed for thinking ahead to her mother's death, even though, taking into account the effect of the gift of Lowca, it was others who should be feeling ashamed.

Sally began to speculate that there might be something more behind all this; perhaps even something sinister. She turned over in her mind, in the course of several sleep-deprived nights, the possibility that Alice inheriting Lowca was the result of animosity towards Sally for something she had done – or perhaps something she had **not** done. Other thoughts surfaced; perhaps she was adopted and her grandmother wasn't actually her grandma; maybe Alice had blackmailed their grandmother.

She could not stop such thoughts racing out of control.

But Sally's foremost thoughts concerned her sister. If the situation had been reversed and the gift had been made to Sally but not to Alice, Sally knew that she would immediately have shared it equally with Alice. Why hadn't **Alice** wanted to share the house?

Her grandmother had been foolish not to have taken advice before writing her Will; and she had been distracted from redoing it by more important things. Sally's mother would have been interfering had she talked to her mother about her Will and might have appeared to be angling to obtain the gift for herself. At most, Sally's mother had merely been ignorant of the possibility that a Will could be amended after death. Who else knew that such a thing was possible? However, nothing at the time helped Sally get over her hurt.

She wondered how much the house in Cumbria might be worth and immediately thought that she was being mercenary.

The only comfort Sally could find in the whole affair was that her grandmother might have been expected to leave all her possessions to her daughter rather than to her granddaughters, in which event Sally would, still, have received nothing on her grandmother's death.

When grandma had come to live with the Bridges in Ashton-under-Lyne, the twins were only four years old, but over the following six years Sally had developed a connection of a kind she had never enjoyed with her mother.

When she first settled down in Ashton-under-Lyne, her grandmother had displayed little warmth towards any of the family; it had even been difficult for Sally to have a proper conversation with her grandmother. Mrs Imber appeared unwell much of the time and was sometimes confused – if not depressed. However, by being patient, by persevering and making regular gestures of kindness towards her grandmother, Sally was able, over time, to get through to her. After six months, her grandmother had thawed and become far less reclusive. She was particularly disposed to spending time with Sally and would never miss their Tuesday evenings together when Alice was having maths tutoring from her mother downstairs.

Sally asked her grandmother lots of questions about her youth. Curiously, her recall of events before the age of ten was exceptional, while thereafter it was abysmal.

Her grandmother was born in London, the youngest of four children. Her three brothers, Jack, Barney and Lou, doted on her, and so she had always felt happy, secure and loved. Whilst her three brothers shared a bedroom, she had her own which she had decorated with her drawings of plants and flowers. Her parents gave her a bicycle when she was five and she spent most of her time after school riding around with her friends Doris Stokes and Christine Puddefeather who lived in the same street.

It was Christine Puddefeather who had taught Sally's grandmother how to play conkers, as a consequence of which she had spent three months in hospital having nearly lost the sight of one of her eyes.

Her grandma once asked Sally to look straight at her. For a child, that had been an unsettling sensation and Sally could recall the conversation:

"I just want you to guess which of my two eyes was the one which was injured."

"It's hard to tell … they are both very beautiful."

"Can't you see anything? Look carefully."

"Hold on … oh yes … your right eye is grey and your left eye is … hazel! How can that be?"

But Sally never did learn which of her grandmother's eyes had been injured or whether the conker accident had caused the different colouration.

There was much else that Sally failed to learn about her grandma. By means of some artful questioning, Sally did, however, ascertain that the whole family had left London when her grandmother was seven. In the weeks leading up to her leaving London, her grandmother had been inconsolable; Doris and Christine were her closest friends and she would likely never see them again.

In her small bedroom, smelling of jasmine, her grandmother would regularly read to Sally. Those reading sessions were the most treasured moments of Sally's early years – and of grandmother's last years. She read to Sally the whole of *'A Tale of Two Cities'* and both *'Emma'* and *'Pride and Prejudice'* and whenever she did not understand a particular word, grandma would stop and explain it. If grandma did not know what it meant then they would both scramble for the well-thumbed dictionary that she kept on her bedside table.

When grandma was not reminiscing with Sally or reading to her, they would play word games. Grandma liked palindromes – her favourite being Napoleon's supposed words: *'Able Was I ere I saw Elba',* but she had joked with Sally that he could not possibly have spoken those immortal words (whether forwards or backwards) since, quite simply, he did not speak English.

Sally's own favourite palindrome, as she never failed to remind her grandmother, was *'Mom's selfless Mom',* although grandma knew that that could not be an accurate description of her – in any direction – nor was it a perfect palindrome because of the occurrence of the apostrophe.

Their favourite word game was called ***DefiniT*** which involved taking a given word and devising some sort of definition of it using each of its letters as the initial letters of that definition. Sally registered that, whilst being boastful was one of the least appropriate qualities which could properly be ascribed to her grandmother, she had often told Sally how pleased she was that she had come up with: 'This Epitomises Nomadic Tribes' – as her *DefiniT* definition of **TENT.**

Playing together in this way afforded grandma and Sally many laughs which were, no doubt, heard by mother and Alice downstairs during their maths lessons. Sally thought that both must have been jealous of the fun going on upstairs without them, as they were always bemused by grandma's ability to enjoy herself.

Whilst Alice hardly spent any time with grandma in her bedroom, Sally was never more content than when she was cossetted in that sweet-smelling environment. Her grandma's room had been a haven for Sally and there was nowhere else in the house she preferred to spend her time, particularly since the bedroom she shared with Alice did not afford much personal space.

The family home was a modest three-bedroom semi-detached house which looked much like it did when it was built in the 1930s; it had the same mantelpieces, the same panelled doors and the same back garden. More significantly, Mr and Mrs Bridge had not made any improvements to the kitchen which still had the same stand-alone gas oven installed by them when they had bought the house. It had never occurred to the Bridges to rip out the familiar old kitchen and install a bright new, all-singing kitchen with an electric oven, rotating corner cabinets, marble splashbacks, flat-panel cabinets with gloss doors and an island installation. They had neglected it much as they had the twins.

13.

A GIFT

Sally had come to learn that many of the problems which beset us (although not the BC problem) might appear at first blush to be more severe than they really are and can often be resolved merely by leaving them be.

And so it was with the turmoil she had been experiencing as a result of the gift of Lowca to Alice, since, over the following weeks, Sally was gradually beginning to notice that the subject was not occupying nearly so much of her waking day. She told herself that she could not claim any attachment to the place; indeed she had not even stayed there overnight.

She could remember seeing chickens in the garden but was not even sure whether this was merely something she had been told about. Sally could remember her grandmother standing at the sink but wondered whether that might have been the sink in their home in Ashton-under-Lyne rather than in Lowca. How was it, Sally questioned, that she could have allowed herself to become so distraught?

The issue did, however, return to the forefront of her mind when she learned of Alice's proposed visit to the UK after an absence of more than three years.

Sally had received an unexpected email from Alice saying that her flight from Istanbul was landing in Manchester at 7pm the following evening and she wanted to know whether Sally could put her up for a few days. Sally busied herself with a grand welcome home dinner, consisting of roast chicken, roast potatoes and broccoli, all liberally seasoned on account of Alice's deficient taste buds. However, because of a delay in take-off, they didn't sit down to eat until after 11pm.

"This is fab, Sally ... Not had a meal like it for years! ... What is this awful wine though."

"Awful? … I see you're on your third glass!"

They both laughed. The truth was, Alice secretly needed it to build up her courage.

"Sally, I have been holding something important from you. I thought it had to wait until I got back from Turkey so we could speak face to face."

Alice looked Sally straight in the eye and engaged in a dramatic pause.

"You can't stop there! What is it? Are you married?" Sally spluttered.

"Yes and no."

"What on earth do you mean?"

*"Yes, I **am** married, but that is only part of what I have been holding back from you."*

"You're pregnant?"

"Er … no; please let me explain. In preparing last week to come back home, I was sorting out my papers, including both my original birth certificate and the copy of yours I took. Well, I happened to notice something astonishing …". Alice paused yet again.

"Yes!?"

*" … it turns out that **you** are the firstborn; not me!"*

Sally went pale with shock, although she did not appreciate the full significance of the revelation at that point. They looked at each other and after a moment's silence they both burst into uncontrollable laughter.

"And all this time," said Sally, *"you have been bullying your big sister*! *When can I get my own back please*?"

They had so much to talk about and Sally felt guilty that she had not yet asked about Alice's husband – she did not even know his name. However, Sally could not even make this the next topic of conversation because, without warning, Alice raised the issue of Lowca.

"Sally, I was dumbstruck when I heard about grandma's gift of her house just to me. I knew there must have been a mistake if you weren't also included in the gift; I did wonder if you had been left something else by grandma and felt so bad when Ma told me this wasn't the case."

Sally was pleased that Alice had raised this because she would have felt it difficult, herself, to have broached it. She was also gladdened that, contrary to the impression that Sally had got from the birthday card, it now appeared that Alice might not be planning to keep Lowca for herself.

Communications hurriedly scribbled on the back of a birthday card are bound to cause misunderstandings, she thought.

"Sally, you must know that there isn't a chance in the world that I would have accepted the gift of grandma's house just for myself. I'm sorry I made you think that. But anyway, that doesn't even matter now ..."

Once again the twins were apparently showing magnanimity towards each other. As a result, the scene was set to allow for the issue to be resolved, quite simply, by the girls agreeing to share the house equally.

A surge of embarrassment gradually overcame Sally as she realised that she had, indeed, so unnecessarily worked herself up over those few words in her sister's twenty-first birthday card ... she had completely overreacted. Had she been more balanced, she told herself, she could have avoided days of needless anxiety and baseless criticism of her family.

Sally did not respond to Alice. Instead, it suddenly dawned on her that she could now resolve two pressing issues which sat together in her in-tray of worries.

First, she could dispel the anxiety she had been experiencing about Alice's selfishness.

Second, she now knew what it was that she would give to Alice by way of the big present for her help with the BC problem. Nothing else would be more appropriate, she thought, than for her to give up any right over their grandmother's home; even though Alice would object. Yes – Lowca would be Sally's grand gesture to Alice and her wedding present as well.

Sally was well aware that her best decisions came from mature reflection rather than reflex reactions and so she resolved to live with her 'perfect solution' before parting with it (and her interest in Lowca).

Unknown to either of them, this would not be as '*grand*' a grand gesture as Sally had supposed since the house was not Sally's to give away. Although it was **Sally** who had now been revealed by Alice as the elder of the twins, it was nevertheless Alice who was technically the rightful owner since their grandmother's bequest had taken effect on her death at a time when it was **Alice** who was acknowledged to be the elder. That issue, however, never came up for discussion between the girls. Nor did it come up for consideration by anyone else because no one, except for Sally and Alice, ever knew of the bizarre reversal of their seniority.

Before Alice could say anything more, Sally changed the subject to talk about Alice's husband. Despite her desperate need for sleep, Alice could not very well resist.

Her husband, Yusef, was actually a friend of the senior official Alice had dated. Sally learnt that the attraction had been instant. Alice took out a few wedding photos that showed he was an imposing man, over six-feet tall, with chiselled features and metal-framed spectacles, little hair but an attractive, though hesitant, smile. Alice enthused. He was a man, she said, who looked after her and always would, no matter where they might finally settle.

Alice apologised shamefacedly that she had not been able to invite Sally to the wedding; it was a source of great regret to her. She told Sally that she had felt very sad that neither Sally nor their parents had been present … she had yet to work out the best way of telling their parents.

Alice explained that the wedding had been planned by Yusef as a surprise for her. The ceremony was a civil one with only his brother and two of their Turkish friends present, after which they had enjoyed a honeymoon weekend in Bodrum. When they had returned home to Istanbul, Alice decided that, seeing that they were coming to England, she would hold back the news and announce it to Sally in person. Yusef had fallen out of favour with the Turkish authorities and, having missed out on several rounds of promotion, he had decided to leave the Ministry of Health and go into civilian life to start a restaurant. Alice explained that this, too, had not worked out and that Yusef would be joining her next week in England.

It transpired that they had little money, not even one job between the two of them and no clear plan as to what they would do with their lives; but Alice was confident that it would not take them long to establish themselves.

It was at this juncture – impulsiveness uncharacteristically getting a hold on her – that Sally put aside her resolution to deliberate on her proposed grand gesture and made her move.

"Alice, you know that I've been worrying about what I might give you as my thankyou for saving me. I have decided – and I don't want any debate – I want you to have the house in Cumbria which will also be my wedding present to you. If you want, you can use it as your home or you could sell it and buy somewhere more

convenient ... whatever you like. I'll have to give notice to Rita's son but both of you could stay here in the meantime."

Sally was expecting Alice to object, but she was too exhausted. There was only much hugging and tears before they each collapsed into bed.

◆ ◆ ◆

It was not easy for Alice and Yusef to set up home in Lowca, having been so used to living in a busy metropolis. They found it hard to make friends with their neighbours – other, that is, than with Rita's son Tom and his wife, who had found a place a few doors up the street. Indeed, for many months that was Alice and Yusef's only friendship and one which seemed to Alice to be all the sweeter for having been passed down by her grandmother.

14.

GRADUATING

The possibility that Sally might not get a position as a *'field operative'* or as a *'non-official cover operative'* (she had already begun researching the possible alternatives) was not all that was causing her melancholia; she was also thinking of *'Alan'* (as she now referred to him) in the ramblings of her mind.

However, Sally had other and more immediate concerns – as did many of her fellow students. She enjoyed law and had decided that she would opt for a career as a solicitor, abandoning the other possibilities such as becoming a barrister. Even if she had the aptitude to stand up in a court (which she knew she did not) the uncertainty of life at the bar would be too much of an obstacle for her – as would be the cost of financing such a venture.

On many occasions (starting in her first academic year) Sally had discussed with her academic adviser the process of seeking an appropriate traineeship and as he grew to appreciate her increased capacity to analyse complex tasks and tackle difficult legal issues with clarity, he upgraded his recommendation to Sally regarding the type of firm which she should aim for, to the point where he was now recommending that she seek a traineeship in one of the big City law firms. She knew that would not be easy, such was the competition. She applied herself to the task the same way as she did for her degree course and went through all the appropriate steps such as sifting those firms which might be best for her, making applications to them well before their cut-off dates and trying to develop an effective interview technique.

As a result, Sally made applications to six City firms and received rejections from all but MacAmbrose Warrior LLP, commonly known as *'MacAmbroses'*. They could hardly go by the name *'Warriors'*, she thought, because that would sound more like a rugby team. Why they had never changed their name was a mystery. There never had been a *'Warrior'* in the firm.

James MacAmbrose had founded the firm two hundred years ago as a one-man business. He had decided that by adding another name (actually, his wife's maiden name) his new firm would appear more substantial. These days, thought Sally, an appearance of substance could be achieved by converting to a limited liability partnership and adding 'LLP' to the name.

MacAmbrose Warrior LLP was regarded as a prestigious firm with a reputation rivalling many of the other top-flight City firms. Its main offices were in Canary Wharf; it had 15 overseas offices, 112 UK partners, 250 solicitors and 60 trainees. It had a wide variety of legal specialisms, including banking, capital markets, competition, corporate, mergers and acquisitions, employment, dispute resolution, intellectual property, insolvency, property and taxation.

Sally had spent a lot of time practising her interview technique, and the two interviews she had with MacAmbroses seemed to go well. She was a little older and that much more mature than most of the other candidates and they offered her a job if she got at least a 2.1 degree and passed the Legal Practice Course.

Sally learned that she had overcome the first of those hurdles.

In the same week, she also received something unexpected, namely, a hand-written letter from Alan Field:

Dear Sally,

Congratulations on your First. Are you still interested in joining us?

AF

Sally was jolted. She had all but decided to banish from her thinking any further ridiculous notions of being involved with the intelligence services; she did not even know anything of what would be required of her.

She wanted stability; nothing in her life seemed to carry with it any kind of security. She lived in temporary student accommodation and she had no job, no money and few friends. She made the decision to forego life as a Bond girl and was surprised how completely at ease she felt with that decision.

She scrunched the letter into a ball and threw it into her wastebin with an elegant flourish, a flourish which was to signal an end to it all.

It was to be pure seduction that brought about a complete reversal of that decision.

Sally had enjoyed playing basketball in her last year of university but had little time for that now – or, indeed, for anything – with the Legal Practice Course facing her. This was to start in September at the Moorgate campus and would be her last set of formal exams prior to starting her traineeship.

On the morning on which that course was to start, Alan Field was waiting for her outside her flat.

"Can I get the bus with you to Moorgate?"

Sally was seriously discomfited both by his words and his unexpected resurfacing. She was, yet again, rendered speechless by him. A mixture of feelings overcame her: outrage that he should appear out of the blue; puzzlement that he knew she was going to take the bus to Moorgate; anger that he had assumed, after more than eighteen months, that she might still want to talk to him or was still available or willing to join the intelligence services; and disgust that his words contained no suggestion of an apology.

Without answering him, she started walking towards the bus stop, Alan Field following behind her. This was the first occasion since they had met each other that she had taken the initiative; she knew it was an insignificant gesture, but it made her feel better.

"How did you know that I would be taking the bus this morning?"

"I just guessed. I know you like buses."

"Why has it taken so long for you to get back into contact with me?"

Alan scratched his ear. *"Look, I know that we have been short on communication, but I will make up for it."*

The number 21 arrived and Alan followed Sally upstairs to the back of the bus. *"We work on the basis that we avoid any communications other than those which are strictly necessary. In that way, there is less risk of interception; I hope you understand. I don't in any way take it for granted that you are still interested; in fact, that is why I turned up this morning to talk to you. I will fully accept it if you have moved on. By the way, congratulations again on your First."*

The bus was now full and all this was said in a whisper. She could smell his breath, and it was sweet.

Sally turned to look at him and their faces almost touched.

"I am not interested, Alan, and I don't want to waste any more of your time."

"I fully respect that, but it would be a great pity for you to make that decision without my explaining a little more. Would you, at least, have supper with me tonight, say at 8pm at Tapas Pasta? You know the place; it's at the bottom of your road."

Alan Field did not get an answer. They reached Moorgate and Sally walked purposefully down the stairs and got off the bus.

She had a lot of thinking to do and only ten hours or so to reach a decision. She walked down the Strand to Victoria Embankment Gardens to clear her mind.

She had originally decided on a definite 'yes' and had moved, just a week ago, to a definite 'no'. She hated being asked to decide again. Sally knew that were she not to turn up at Tapas Pasta that evening then that would certainly be the end of the matter for, even if she were subsequently to change her mind, she would not be able to locate Alan Field to tell him.

As Sally continued turning things over in her thoughts in the hope of producing some solid conclusion, a definite 'maybe' was beginning to creep into the mix.

Her life was boring; she had still never left these shores and she had never had a boyfriend. What was she doing with her life? She had not for a long time been taken out by anyone. But, she thought, if Alan really wanted to ensure that she would have dinner with him that evening, why had he not offered to call for her? Did he think that by giving her the space to decline his clumsy invitation she would be more likely to accept it?

Sally did not need the whole 10 hours (or even one of them) to decide what she was going to do although that decision was one which troubled her exceedingly.

Alan Field knew that he had played his hand exquisitely; like an experienced angler, he was reeling in his catch. In the fishing lake of life, Sally was out of her depth – she was more a rash bass than a canny carp.

And so it was that Sally did decide to meet Alan Field that evening at *Tapas Pasta*, a quirky restaurant with an identity crisis. Her only concession was to arrive 10 minutes late.

They had a lot to eat, to drink and to talk about. Alan avoided any reference to the intelligence services although Sally tried on several occasions to steer the conversation in that direction. He did, however, mention that he had recently been to South America which, he said, was one of the reasons he had not been in touch. It was odd, Sally thought, that while telling her this he had his face cupped in his hands as if he were wearing a mask.

Alan was very attentive and asked Sally a lot of questions of the kind you might put if you were interested in building a relationship with someone rather than the intrusive questions a prospective employer or doctor might ask. He was, throughout, kind and considerate and nothing he asked Sally gave her reason to feel any awkwardness or embarrassment.

They were the last to leave the restaurant that evening and Alan said he would walk Sally home. As they reached her street he stopped abruptly and turned towards her.

"*Sally …,*" he prefaced, followed by a very long pause, "*… there is something I have to tell you …*" and then another long pause. He was clearly hesitant in coming out with it.

"*… my real name is Anthony Forth – Tony Forth.*"

Sally did not respond. She merely smiled at him and walked the rest of the short distance to her flat on her own.

The disclosure that Alan Field was not really Alan Field was the first time he had revealed anything about himself to Sally. She felt more privileged than deceived. It was no great surprise to Sally since secret agents could hardly operate in secrecy if they were to use their real names – but how was she to know that he did not own a third nom de plume or perhaps a dozen or so? Sally decided that she did not care. She found '*Tony Forth*' (or whatever his name was) attractive and she would be prepared to address him using any name.

Within a month Sally and Tony were seeing each other most days and, in another three months, Sally had given up her place and was living with Tony in his two-bedroom ground floor flat in Mildmay Road. It was Sally who had proposed the move, motivated, she told Tony, by the prospect of saving rent on her flat and having a shorter journey to Moorgate.

In the meantime, although Alice had learned from her phone conversations with Sally that she had a boyfriend, Sally had revealed only very few details about Tony and Alice was intrigued to meet him. Sally suggested that she should come to London and they eventually found a convenient date.

Sally met Alice at Euston Station full of embarrassment. Tony had been called abroad only three hours earlier and so Alice had to make do with listening to Sally's account of the man. This was not easy for either of them since Sally had no photos of him, no convincing account of what Tony actually did as an international oil trader, no knowledge of Tony's friends, merely a sketchy outline of his family; and she was not even sure of his name.

It was surprising to Sally that the wily Alice had not tumbled to the conclusion that Tony was working for the intelligence services, although at one point during the course of the evening Alice did ask Sally whether Tony was merely a creature of her imagination, at which, in an effort to show that she had not taken leave of her senses, Sally announced that she had just moved in with him.

*"You've what? You've only just met him. I had known Yusef for fifteen months before we started living together! You obviously don't know anything about the guy and he is obviously completely unreliable. What **are** you doing?"*

"Don't get so heated. We're only living together – we're not getting married. Alice, I really do think that I'm doing the right thing … I am so happy in his company. He looks after me. And he loves me. What better reasons can there be for two people to live together?"

Alice, begrudgingly, said that she understood. But her mission to London had been rendered essentially pointless, and she was disgruntled.

"I'm sure you would understand more, Alice, if you spent some time in his company. I'm arranging a 30th birthday lunch for Tony on 20th March … you must come."

It was to be a small birthday lunch in a local pub with only Alice, their parents, Doreen Okanwe and a friend of Tony, Alex Carstairs. However, Alice did not acknowledge receipt of the invitation – nor did she even apologise for failing to attend.

Despite Tony's conviviality during the lunch and several bottles of good wine, the conversation was strained. Once the introductions had been made and pleasantries exchanged, it transpired that Tony had little in common with Sally's parents and pools of silence constantly dampened the occasion. Alex felt awkward and ordered more wine. Doreen spoke mainly to Sally's father about politics. Her infectious laughter showed that at least she was enjoying the lunch. '*Oh, for Alice!*' thought Sally as Tony was making yet another valiant effort to engage with Sally's mother.

Sally became increasingly distracted as the meal went on; she was resentful of Alice for her obvious snub. At one point, she made a bid to engage Alex in the hope of shaking off her gloom; she hoped to pick up a few tidbits regarding Tony, however, he was not forthcoming – in fact, from whatever angle Sally approached him, whether she talked about him or Tony, he said little.

Alex described himself as an old friend of Tony, but the most she could get out of him was that, as a kid on holiday with his parents in Canada, Tony had saved his parents from the clutches of a brown bear by throwing a groundsheet over it. She asked Alex whether he had travelled much with Tony, to which he glibly and annoyingly answered *'only on the Central Line'* and changed the subject. She decided that she did not like Alex. Even if his calling imposed limits on what he was free to say to her, he did not have to insult her intelligence.

In the cab on the way home, Sally told Tony how she felt; how she thought that the lunch had been a failure; but Tony did not agree, and he told her not to fret about Alex's behaviour – Alex was always evasive. That clipped response, coming as it did from someone who could, himself, hardly be described as garrulous, did not pacify her. Indeed, it made things worse, since it fuelled her growing awareness that Tony had still shown no inclination to open up to Sally.

❖ ❖ ❖

It was July and, having just successfully completed the Legal Practice Course, Sally was at home in Mildmay Road recovering when the doorbell rang. Tony was not at home. At the front door was a red-headed man in his early fifties wearing a dark navy suit, white shirt, cufflinks and a red Windsor-knotted tie. He was clean shaven, immaculately coiffured and described himself as a colleague of Tony. He apologised for interrupting her but wondered whether she could spare him half an hour. She was not prepared to let a stranger into the flat, and he, picking up on this, asked her whether they might walk along the street to talk. Sally was equally uncertain about going off with a stranger, even if it was in a busy street in daylight, however, it crossed her mind that something might have happened to Tony, and she did not feel that she could simply turn the man away without finding out why he had called.

"Tell me one thing that will prove you are a work colleague of Tony."

He paused.

*"Well, it's not exactly a **work** thing but an idiosyncrasy,"* he replied, *"Tony sometimes has the habit, right in the middle of a conversation with you, of hiding his face by cupping it in his two hands. It is rather off-putting … does that help at all?"*

She grabbed her wallet and keys and walked with him the five minutes to a coffee shop on the Kingsland Road, where they installed themselves at a table in the corner.

"I am sorry. I haven't even properly introduced myself. As I mentioned, I work with Tony, and my name is Jonathan Jones, but you can call me 'JJ'."

He had a pleasant smile and a soft Australian accent. He leant forward and spoke again, this time very quietly.

"If my dropping by unannounced has caused you the slightest bit of concern then do please forgive me. Why I came around was to tell you that we would still like to extend to you the opportunity of working with us ..."

He did not wait for a response.

"... What we need are operatives in large firms of solicitors who can alert us if they spot circumstances which might indicate that clients may be involved in money laundering, particularly by or for the benefit of terrorists. We are not really interested in money laundering itself, but it has proved a useful angle and we have developed an early warning system that can identify a dozen or so occurrences or transactions which may indicate that money laundering by terrorists is going on. Firms have excellent systems in place and they do a really good job of inhibiting this kind of pernicious behaviour, but we can't expect them to act as detectives."

He paused, gulped down the rest of his coffee and continued with even greater enthusiasm.

"In our experience, trainees move from seat to seat in different departments and so sometimes have a better opportunity to spot money laundering. It's odd that this should be so, isn't it? You would not expect in any

business that a rookie newcomer might be able to spot things that their bosses might not. It is completely counter-intuitive."

"That does not seem straightforward. Would I be trained?"

*"Yes, **I** would be the person doing the training and I would be your point of contact. It would be sensible, now you and Tony are together, that your Official Secrets confidentiality obligations extend also to communications between you both."*

"Would MacAmbrose Warrior know all about this?""Oh, of course. We would speak to the Senior Partner; they would approve your involvement, although I should add that it is more than possible that throughout your time there you will have nothing to do."*

"Is there a name in the Service for this kind of work?"

There was a pause, and Sally detected a mild reaction from JJ. Maybe his coffee went down the wrong way.

"We call such an agent a 'JIE' or a Junior Intelligence Executive. The rate for JIEs is not high. You would get £750 per month before tax. I will call you in a week's time to see if you are still interested. We don't have anyone at MacAmbroses at present. Thanks so much for talking to me, but I must run."

They shook hands and he was off.

That evening, Sally raised with Tony whether she should accept such a position with the security services. Tony said he did not think she should since circumstances were now very different from what they were some two and a half years ago when he had first recruited her. Sally nevertheless passionately argued that she would like to do her bit for *'Queen and Country',* and the whole idea of working for MI5, even if at a lowly level, would be an exciting opportunity in a life which, up till now, she felt had been distinctly uninspiring and lacking in adventure.

"Bloody hell, Tony, I haven't even been out of the country!"

"You are obviously keen and if this is what you really want then I wouldn't stand in your way."

The following week when JJ called, she told him that she would like to accept his offer of becoming a JIE and he called round later to deal with the paperwork including signing the Official Secrets Act commitment. There would be a series of training sessions the first of which was scheduled for the following week.

Sally spent the next hour writing notes in her black notebook of everything that had taken place that day between JJ and herself. Tony, scribbling away in his own notebook, remarked offhandedly to Sally and without looking up at her that he was impressed that her four years of legal study were, at last, appearing to pay off.

.

15.
TRAINEESHIP

The following week, Sally was invited to attend a three-afternoon training sessions given by JJ in a private suite in a hotel in Bloomsbury, WC1. There were two other trainees sitting at small tables directly in front of Sally one of whom was a tall blonde with a prominent streak of pink hair stretching from the back of her neck right across the top of her head.

JJ explained that, for confidentiality purposes, the identity of the trainees would not be released nor should they converse with each other. This was an unsettling experience for Sally, since it had been natural for her to compare notes – and no opportunity had been built into the timetable to facilitate that. JJ must have appreciated that these restrictions were unusual, however, Sally thought they created an aura of secrecy which made her feel important.

Extraordinarily, JJ told the three trainees that, at the close of each day, they would have to leave the hotel lecture room one by one, at five-minute intervals.

Beginning his introduction to the course, JJ explained that unintentionally allowing or facilitating money laundering was a serious risk for all professional concerns and that, despite vigorous efforts by law enforcement agencies to combat such risk, they were finding that criminal minds around the world were coming up with increasingly sophisticated strategies to side-step their efforts. This was particularly pernicious where such strategies were being employed by terrorists. Only careful vigilance would help to stop money laundering.

He explained that combatting money laundering was not the function of the security service, however, monitoring it was often a 'backdoor' entry method for detecting terrorism and locating terrorists.

He went on to say that money laundering was sometimes difficult to identify. Over the three afternoons, JJ covered some of the '*red flags*' which, if spotted in good time, could lead to opportunities to uncover terrorist networks.

Sally made a note of the many kinds of suspicious behaviour to look out for:

- **a reluctance on the part of a client to provide adequate information;**
- **a transfer of money where there is no indication of a plausible business relationship between the parties;**
- **a proposed transfer of funds into a firm's client account without legitimate reason;**
- **a client being prepared to give instructions only through an intermediary;**
- **instructions coming from a client in a place which has no geographic connection to the firm; and**
- **a sudden settlement of litigation or the falling through of a deal, suggesting that the initial instructions might merely have been a ploy to get money into a firm's client account.**

JJ worked through each of the scenarios, giving detailed practical examples. Sally thought that of all the tuition she had received on the subject of anti-money laundering, this course had been the most useful despite there being no opportunity to ask questions. At the end of the third afternoon, there was a short burst of applause.

Three weeks later, Sally started her traineeship at MacAmbrose Warrior LLP in their offices on the thirteenth, fourteenth and fifteenth floors of an impressive tower block in Canary Wharf. The twenty-five new trainees spent the first week on an induction course, run with military precision and covering every aspect of the firm's systems and operations. It began with a basic welcome from the Senior Partner who put a lot of emphasis on the firm's ethos and standards.

This was followed by a tour of the office, led by a second-year trainee, indicating where in the building each main department of the firm was situated. It included the main library, the research assistants' room, client meeting rooms, board rooms, the accounting and finance department, the human resources offices, the marketing section, the compliance office, the post room, the file storage and the records room; the receptionists' desk, the secretarial suites, the security office, the document production office; the restaurant, gym and two overnight accommodation rooms.

There was a basic introduction to the firm's internal intranet, containing vast tracts of data which would take months (if not longer, Sally thought) to assimilate.

They would need to learn things such as how to maintain client confidentiality; how to use the internet in compliance with office rules; how to use the telephone system; how to open client files; how to record time spent on client matters and office work; how the billing system works; how to access the accounts package; how to search for details of members of staff; how to record personal employment details; recover expenses; carry out searches; locate files and a host of other matters including the firm's anti-discrimination policy; the office rules requiring the disclosure of personal relationships both within and outside the firm; how to address partners and each other; how to dress for work; and the house rules dealing with the expected norms of behaviour between fellow members of the firm.

And then there were the firm's arrangements for continuing education; the rules for avoiding conflicts of interests and, finally, the firm's rules regarding insider dealing.

Even though this had merely been a gentle introductory course, by the end of the week, Sally was exhausted. Manuals covering the week's peregrinations were handed out to the trainees with the inference that this was their weekend work – not that the next two years would be anything other than a seamless stretch of time where weekends, holidays and the midnight pips would assume little relevance in the journey of a trainee. Such was the way of most of the City law firms.

Sally's first '*seat*' was in Dispute Resolution, otherwise known as litigation. Her initial job was to help prepare the bundles of documents required for a trial which was to start the following week. Together with Ben Ashcrofte, who had also just started as a trainee, Sally had to ensure that each of the twelve copies of a 215-page Witness Statement were numbered in exactly the same way so that it would be possible for all those involved in the court proceedings to refer to it effectively. If there were any discrepancies in the pagination of any trial document, the judge could halt the trial until the pages had been correctly renumbered. The extra costs involved would be borne by the party in default which, in turn, meant that its solicitors would have to pick up the tab.

Sally proved efficient at this task and (although she was not expected to do so) she was able to read large chunks of the Witness Statement at the same time as checking the pagination, which led to her noticing a contradiction. It seemed that the executive making the Statement would have had to have been in two separate meetings, 120 miles apart, at the same time and she passed that observation onto the partner concerned. Failing to notice this could have called into question the credibility of what that executive had to say in his Statement and that could have been embarrassing for the client as well as for MacAmbroses.

After the trial had ended, Sally was brought in to help out on a claim concerning a cleaning services company. One of its two owner/directors (the defendant) was being sued for breach of duty by the other owner/director (the claimant) who claimed that the defendant had improperly diverted contracts from the company to another company secretly owned by the defendant. The facts were hotly contested and the claimant promised to provide MacAmbroses with the evidence to back up his claim. That eagerly awaited evidence, once delivered, was, however, most disappointing since it consisted of more than fifteen hundred loose dog-eared letters, emails and hand-written notes compressed into one large dusty unforgiving suitcase. It fell to Sally to sort out that mess and make sense of it.

Sally spent most of her time sitting in on meetings with clients and was sometimes given the task of taking detailed notes. After one particularly long meeting, Sally found, four days later, that she had mislaid both her original manuscript notes and the cassette containing the notes she had dictated. Seeing that the minutes of the meeting were required for a meeting early the following morning, she had no alternative but to stay at the office until 2am in order to produce a new set of notes. Luckily for her, no one became aware she had lost her notes and there was nothing to deter the firm from subsequently giving her more responsibility.

She was asked to prepare the first draft of instructions to the barrister advising a client on a high-profile privacy case involving the leaking of private letters and was frequently involved in preparing affidavits for clients to present their evidence to court.

With there being so much to do each day and so many competing forces, learning how to juggle became important. Sally reminded herself of the mantra *'a trainee who fails to recognise priorities will fail to be recognised.'*

One of the priorities in a solicitor's office was continuing education and Sally knew she could not miss any training sessions, even if she thought she knew it all, such as the in-house training session on anti-money laundering from which her fellow trainees came away most impressed at how much Sally knew.

Sally allowed herself to be side-tracked during that session and found herself concentrating on the **wording** of the title of the training session rather than on its substance. There was something odd, she thought, about the words *'anti-money laundering'*, where the hyphen occurred **before** *'money'*, whereas she would have expected the hyphen to appear, instead, between *'money'* and *'laundering'*. At least that was the practice in similar compounds such as *'money-saving'*. However, no one seemed to adopt that style in the phrase *'money laundering'*. Sally decided she could live with that but found it difficult to accept that, as a result of the hyphen transfer, the phrase *'anti-money laundering'* seemed to suggest that it had something to do with an anarchist practice advocating the abolition of money.

During the whole six months spent as a trainee, the constant effort required of Sally meant that she found it hard to switch off from her MacAmbrose work. Tony understood this and, whenever possible, they chose their downtime carefully so that they could enjoy it together.

Early one morning before she had left for work, Sally was interrupted by an unexpected telephone call from JJ. He asked her if she could find out the number of charities the firm had helped to establish in the past year and who in the firm was the most experienced in registering new charities. Sally – eager to impress on this, her first assignment in the security service – called JJ that evening on the phone with her responses. He thanked her and was gone without any niceties.

Somewhat late in the day, Sally began to reflect on what had just happened. This was not, she realised, the kind of assignment she had expected to undertake in her role with the services. She thought that being asked to report to MI5 on clients who appeared to be committing a breach of anti-money laundering laws might be in the public interest. However, she did not understand the relevance of being asked to report on charities. She shook her head slowly in self-disbelief as a sudden apprehensiveness came over her. She thought that she might have been so very stupid. However, the morning brought some calmer reflection; the Senior Partner had approved her clandestine appointment and so she should not be concerned about its propriety.

Over the next few weeks Sally managed to cope with her discomposure by injecting even more effort into her work at MacAmbroses to the point where she was beginning to be noticed as a star in the ascendancy, and no sooner had she walked into the trainee's room one morning than Ben Ashcrofte strode over to tell her that the Senior Partner had been looking for her.

Worries will often accumulate clandestinely, over time, in our subconscious and, having built up sufficient mass, formulate some uneasiness which sooner or later develops into a serious apprehension – all the while without any permission from our conscious mind. And so it was with Sally. Having accepted JJ's statement that MacAmbroses would approve her involvement in M15, it occurred to her, out of the blue, that nothing had occurred to give her any confidence that any such approval had even been requested. If it had been requested, she could safely assume that her involvement had been approved; otherwise she would not have been taken on as a trainee. However, she began to have serious misgivings as to whether the firm was aware of her '*extra role*'. Perhaps there had been an administrative error; maybe JJ had forgotten to deal with this. Those misgivings multiplied when she tried to put herself in the position of the Senior Partner of the firm. If he **had** been contacted by M15 surely, at some point, he would have wished to make some contact with Sally? She had worked in the firm for six months and she had not received so much as a nod **or** a wink from anyone.

And so an urgent summons from the Senior Partner, whom she had met only on the induction day six months ago, was an occasion for concern. Would this, Sally asked herself, be the occasion for a nod, a wink or something else?

Sally marched briskly to the Senior Partner's office. He was not there when she arrived and so she waited, feeling with each minute an increase in her blood pressure.

When the Senior Partner returned, he ushered her into his spacious office and without asking her to take one of the many chairs around his desk, he requested her to wait while he made a short call.

"*I am concerned ... ,*" he said slowly and deliberately, "*... that none of the trainees in my department are currently available to assist me on an important matter. I know you are busy doing a job for Derek, but I've had a word with him and he's OK for you to drop everything to help me out ... Basically I've got six hours to prepare an urgent report which my clients need to receive by tonight so that they can decide whether to go ahead with an acquisition they are involved in. Let me give you this Memo which explains all you need ... Here's the name of the client and the matter number so you can fill out your time sheet.*"

And with a nod of the head (but no wink) he was gone. There was no thank you, but the economy and speed with which he had imparted his instructions and the fact that he had not asked Sally whether she had any questions were sufficient to give her the warm feeling that he had complete confidence in her ability to complete what seemed to her to be a critical piece of work.

The job involved considering the merits of a trade mark application for the name '*Pedals*', used by a company that had been selling bicycles for 30 years. Another company, which had been manufacturing bicycles for even longer had objected to the grant of that trade mark, and Sally's task was to report on whether the opposition to that application was likely to succeed. The issue, as Sally set out in her Report, depended on '*some nice distinctions*', where one of two equally deserving parties had to suffer.

She got stuck into the job immediately, finding a similar court case decided in 2001 involving two confectionery companies, both of which had been producing confectionery using the trade name '*Refreshers*'. Sally referred to that authority in preparing the first draft of her Report which she managed to deliver to the Senior Partner well within the six-hour deadline. He took it on from there saying that he was very pleased with the work which Sally had done – and so was Sally.

When she got back to the flat that evening, Sally found Tony relaxing on the sofa with a newspaper and a glass of red wine and listening (so he told her) to Haydn's Piano Trio No. 25 in E Minor. He was, indeed, more relaxed than she had seen him for weeks.

After pouring herself, by way of a reward, a larger glass of wine than she would normally have allowed herself, she sat down next to Tony and kissed him.

He asked whether she had had a good day and she told him how pleased the Senior Partner had been with her work. When Tony enquired further, she gave him the briefest of outlines but without mentioning any names – although she did let slip the name of the trade mark.

"Do you think your client will win?"

"I don't know," she replied, *"it's not our clients who are actually applying for the trade mark; they are only investigating to help them decide whether to proceed with an acquisition of some sort."*

16.
BUS NUMBER 277

Tony had left the flat early the following morning and so Sally decided that she, too, would make an early start.

From the top of the number 277 bus as it travelled along Victoria Park Road, Sally caught a glimpse of Tony walking along the street. She was about to tap on the window, but he would never have heard her. Nor would it have been sensible for Sally to attract his attention because it was apparently already focused on a blonde. Sally immediately recognised her as one of her two co-students at JJ's anti-money laundering course – at least she thought it was her because of the prominent streak of pink hair.

This image occupied Sally the whole day, which, in consequence, was not a productive one. She left the office early and on the way home received a text from Tony saying that he would not be coming home that evening.

And so Sally was left to fret over thoughts of Tony's infidelity with only a lacklustre pizza and a glass of wine for distraction.

Thinking about her relationship with Tony, Sally realised that although this had not deepened much since they had moved in together, she did (despite his curious ways) feel a lot for him. She had regularly experienced pangs of jealousy and had not had enough confidence in the robustness of their relationship to be able to ignore the sidelong glances that Tony regularly squandered on women when they were out together. She had told herself that such glances indicated little more than the innocent eye-wandering antics that all men indulge in when an attractive woman comes into their line of sight. She compared it to the occasions her head was turned by some Adonis.

Their sex life gave Sally much satisfaction and Tony's companionship made her feel cocooned. He had a good sense of humour and (on occasions) he would have plenty to talk to her about.

However, there was something which concerned Sally more than anything else; it was that Tony appeared to have few friends, little family and hardly any recollection (at least which he was prepared to share with her) regarding his life before meeting her. Tony was always so coy about his youth and his family. Why should such an apparently gregarious fellow have next to no friends? Sally often felt that it was as if Tony was holding back – holding back from committing himself to her. She had decided that, whether or not it was a conscious thought process on his part, Tony had decided that breaking up with her would be easier if he were to tell her as little as possible about himself.

She also wondered whether his holding back might even be more sinister. Perhaps Tony had something dark in his past that he was keeping to himself.

Added to this goulash of concerns about her relationship with Tony was the fact that he spent days at a time away from the flat 'on business' without ever making any effort to account for them. Of course, that might all be explained by the rigours of his job and its strict discipline and Sally told herself that she was being foolish if she expected Tony to account for where he had been on Monday or why he would not be coming home next Saturday.

She told herself that she was proud of what he was and proud of what he was doing.

However, that did not prevent her thoughts coming to settle on another worry about Tony, and one which had gradually grown in intensity, so adding even more fuel to the fire of her growing feeling of discomfort. Explaining Tony's secretiveness as a natural function of being an MI5 operative was one thing, but Sally was also harbouring the concern that there might be another more plausible explanation, namely, that Tony was **not** an MI5 operative. This thought made her feel sick. It would mean JJ had to be in on it as well. It was a ridiculous notion but Sally could not altogether banish the possibility. Why should MI5 have an interest in money laundering when other agencies had far better resources to deal with this particular area of law enforcement?

Sally's mind continued to race erratically from one premonition of misfortune to another; none of them, she realised, bearing any evidence. She told herself that this was all surmise, which was made worse as a consequence of her being a consummate worrier and she reminded herself of all the unnecessary angst she had allowed to build up out of those scribbled words on her 21st birthday card from Alice. She gave a little shudder by way of acknowledgement of how very stupid she had been on that occasion.

A good night's sleep helped Sally to put aside these morose thoughts.

She had been asked to spend the day at the High Court in the Strand to take detailed notes of a judgment to be handed down by the Court of Appeal on a case concerning a series of share transfers in a private company. It was argued by MacAmbroses' client, a Mr Peacock, that those transfers had been made in breach of the company's articles of association, which required the shares, first, to be offered to him. It was a tedious day, but Sally enjoyed listening to the proceedings; they certainly took her mind off the worries of the previous night.

After the case was finished (with Mr Peacock losing his appeal), Sally decided to go home early. She took the bus home to Dalston and, being totally occupied working on her notes, did not get round to reading her *Evening Standard*.

As soon as she arrived home and before even taking off her shoes, she went into the kitchen to see what food there was in the freezer for that evening. The first thing that caught her eye was a brown envelope propped up against a half-empty can of lager on the table. She opened the envelope to find a large number of £50 notes.

Sally's first thought was that this was some kind of prank or maybe a stunt to test her. Perhaps they were forged banknotes. She was perplexed and looked around for some indication of what this stash might signify. No one leaves large sums of cash around without a reason, she kept on saying to herself. She counted the notes; there were ninety-nine of them – just under £5,000.

She picked up the brown envelope to see if she had missed anything and inside it, half the size of a credit card, was a scrappy piece of newsprint torn unevenly from a newspaper with some hastily scribbled words in the margin: *'I'm sorry '*.

It was definitely Tony's handwriting.

Sally clutched the scrap of paper in desperation and now knew this could be neither a joke nor some MI5 initiative test. She went cold. Did this mean that Tony had left her?

She called JJ but there was no reply.

She wanted to call someone else who could tell her the truth, but the truth was that there was no one else who could help her.

She ran into their bedroom.

She tempestuously pulled open all of Tony's wardrobes and cupboards. His two best suits were missing. So was his iPad. And so was his small suitcase. Tony must have returned to the flat after she had left for work that morning.

She knew that it was pointless for her to deny the worst. For a few minutes, Sally kept calm even though her world and her self-esteem were in the process of crumbling in front of her.

Then she panicked. She lost control. She was angry. She was angry with Tony for everything; for seducing her into his bed; for inveigling her into MI5; and angry that he had now gone off without even saying goodbye – or, indeed, without ever having properly said hello to her.

Sally stumbled blindly towards the kitchen table, where she grabbed a handful of £50 notes and began, frenziedly, tearing them and, if unable to tear them, crumpling them into as small as possible units of loathing. She ran around the kitchen flinging the notes around in disgust – an effort which temporarily calmed her. She slumped into a kitchen chair and began thumping the table violently, using both fists in tandem, her anger gradually building a head of steam.

If he had ever had the slightest affection or respect for her then, surely, he would have given her a proper explanation of what was behind his leaving her. Without any such explanation his pathetic apology was a hollow one for which he deserved nothing but her utter contempt.

She moved from anger at him to disgust with herself – she could not believe that she had allowed herself to fall in love with such a man.

She was consumed by a fog – a fog of abject loneliness – with the realisation that, apart from Alice (who was in Lowca), the only friend to whom she could turn was Doreen (who was now in Nigeria). Even Alice would hardly be a suitable confidante, since at some point she would be certain to utter those four words which no one wants to hear – *"I told you so!"*

What had existed in her jumbled thoughts only twenty-four hours earlier merely as a nagging doubt had now been recast into a stark reality, for she was certain that Tony had exited from her life.

Even if he were to reappear, she would not be able to have any further connection with a man who had behaved in the base-minded, contemptible manner which he had.

The same question kept coming back to her – as a bad dream to a troubled soul – why had he left her and why in this manner?

It made no sense to her, particularly when she recollected the paradigm of domesticity she had enjoyed with Tony the previous evening. She began to go through everything that he had said to her in the search for some plausible explanation, some clue as to what had happened – or maybe nothing *new* had happened and Tony's hasty departure had been planned for a long while.

Could the reason have been something to do with what Sally had done or not done? Had it merely been some emergency at work which had given rise to him leaving her so urgently?

It occurred to her that she might never find out whether Tony had been working with MI5, because she convinced herself that she would never see him again.

And that brought Sally to another line of thought. If Tony's post in MI5 (or even in any ersatz

MI5) did have something to do with his departure, could this have any repercussions for her job at MacAmbroses? Was this an appropriate time for her to say something to the Senior Partner?

Sally needed to remind herself of JJ's precise words when he told her that M15 would clear her appointment with MacAmbroses and she went into the kitchen to fetch her black notebook. When she found that that too was missing (no doubt taken by Tony) she was finally certain of the sorry truth even though, by now, she hardly needed any further confirmation of it.

She knew that she could not stay in the flat a moment longer. But where could she go? Who could she visit at 5.00pm on a Wednesday afternoon?

She decided, on impulse, that the best environment for clearing her mind would be her workplace, the familiarity of which, together with the comradeship it brought, would soothe her. Somehow she managed to put on fresh make-up and get the bus back to work.

The motion of the bus helped her to recover a little. She kept her eyes closed for most of the journey but was rendered fully alert when she opened them and noticed the headlines in the business section of the *Evening Standard*, held aloft by the man on the seat directly in front of her – *'Conjoined Securities rides away with United Pedals.'*

As she glanced at the headline she barely registered its significance. However, within a millisecond she was stricken by the overwhelming realisation that she was staring at the very truth for which she had been searching; a realisation which caused Sally to feel sick to the core of her being.

There was no explanation that could have been worse for Sally, but it was the only explanation of all the possible candidates which could make any sense to her.

Sally looked up just in time to see that her stop in Canary Wharf was approaching, and she automatically started to move towards the stairs to get off the bus. She stopped herself. She realised that she had a lot more thinking to do before she could face going back to the office and in her present state she could envisage nowhere better than the front of the top deck of the number 277 London Transport double decker red bus, which was now heading (with her) in the opposite direction to MacAmbroses.

It was now clear to Sally that Tony had disappeared because he had fathomed the significance of the '*Pedals*' trade mark which she had accidentally divulged the previous evening. No doubt he was already enjoying the substantial profit he would have made from using that insider information. Perhaps he, himself, had bought shares in United Pedals plc or perhaps he had sold on the information to someone else.

Indeed, although Sally could not have known it, the innocent piece of information regarding '*Pedals*' which she had provided to Tony had been enough for him to buy 3.2m shares in United Pedals plc at 99.7p per share and to sell them that same morning at 200.6p per share, netting a profit on the deal of over £3m. The proceeds, in short, were held in a Cayman Islands company, but not for long.

Sally did not know much about the law of insider trading. She had merely touched on it at LSE and had not yet been required to look at it during her time at MacAmbroses. But she knew three things – it was easy to fall foul of the legislation; the penalties were severe with up to 7 years' imprisonment; and it was an offence to pass insider information to another person.

She had heard it said that it was a victimless crime, but she knew enough to realise that could be a dangerous over-simplification, since for any stock exchange to operate effectively, it must have the confidence of all those who invest in it. That confidence was vital to the effective working of the City – and also to the existence of Sally's job at MacAmbroses.

She knew that any trade of the kind that Tony might have carried out would be identified as suspicious and that it would certainly be reported to the FCA for investigation. That investigation would inevitably involve MacAmbroses and, through them, anyone in the firm who had spent time working on the *Pedals* deal, including even the meagre three hours spent by her. If it came out that Tony had profited from any dealing in those shares it would not be long before his connection to Sally would be identified.

Sally kept asking herself whether she should keep these thoughts to herself or whether she should own up to what could be seen as a minor indiscretion – a mere slip of the tongue – where she had not intended to obtain (nor **had** she obtained) any benefit for herself. Owning up now would certainly avoid the all-pervasive feeling of apprehension she knew she would otherwise experience every day of her traineeship if she were to decide to keep things to herself. In any event,

Sally did not think she could manage the stress of failing to disclose what had happened – she would indefinitely be looking over her shoulder, hoping that her connection with Tony Forth would not come to light.

On the other hand, how could she even contemplate deciding to come clean when her worst fears continued to be based merely on assumptions – she had no concrete evidence of anything?

Her mind was in turmoil as it navigated from one foreboding to the next then settling once again on Tony. She felt that Tony's was the basest form of treachery because if his leaving her **was** out of naked greed, this to Sally would be far worse than if he had left her for another woman.

She looked out of the window of the number 277; she had arrived at the Isle of Dogs.

She immediately boarded another number 277 bus travelling back in the direction she had just journeyed and as soon as she arrived at MacAmbroses, she marched, as if impelled, to the Senior Partner, hoping he would be in his office:

"Good evening Sally, what is it I can do for you?"

"May I sit down and talk to you? I will need a good half hour."

"It's that serious, eh?" he joked. *"By all means. Please sit down."*

"I am afraid that I have been very stupid, in two respects and I am not quite sure how to begin. Way back in September 2010, I was recruited by MI5, or at least I thought I had been."

Sally paused and concentrated hard on the Senior Partner's face in the hope that there might be some tell or some change in his demeanour which would indicate that he had, all along, known of her covert role in the firm.

But there was none. Instead, there was only an expression of intense irritation bordering on anger. The Senior Partner might have been protecting his own position, but Sally now knew for certain that it would be pointless for her to rely on the firm knowing anything about her undercover role. She became disoriented; she panicked and, in consequence, the confession which poured out from the usually articulate Sally, was reduced to a series of disconnected and incoherent admissions which would merely serve to confuse rather than elicit any kind of compassion or understanding from MacAmbroses.

"I am still not sure whether Tony, the person who recruited me (and with whom I have been living over recent months) is really working for the intelligence services, but that probably doesn't matter for the purposes of this conversation."

The Senior Partner was now beginning to appear as uncomfortable as he was angry. He had not expected this rambling exposé and asked Sally to pause. He told her that he would have to call in the firm's compliance partner and when he came in, five minutes later, Sally had to start all over again, which made what she had to say sound twice as heinous.

Sally continued her rambling:

"Although I have given away two bits of what I think are harmless pieces of firm information regarding charities, I might, unwittingly, have divulged confidential information regarding the United Pedals deal announced this morning. I can't be sure of this, but I mentioned the draft Report I did for you and whilst I didn't mention any names, I did mention the trade mark application to Tony and it is possible that he will put two and two together."

The Senior Partner did not need to hear anything further.

"Miss Bridge ... I cannot believe that you have been so incredibly foolish and so lacking in your duty as an employee of this firm. This is what is going to happen. You will go to the room next door under the scrutiny of my colleague here and you will write out, in the fullest detail possible, all that you have just told us, adding anything else you can recollect, including dates, full names, emails, telephone numbers and addresses. You will then sign that statement and, without returning to your office, you will leave these offices with a security guard ... Goodbye."

Although Sally had expected this treatment, there had been some residual hope in the outer recesses of her mind that the Senior Partner might have wanted to find a way of dealing with this sorry tale in a more sympathetic way. Could they not see her value as one of the firm's newest trainees? She was the young and uninitiated but enormously talented Miss Sally Bridge, who had been duped and made the subject of a perverted conspiracy. She had been sincere and honest when she might have tried to hide her involvement without anyone ever coming to know the true facts. It was her belief, therefore, that MacAmbrose Warrior LLP should, if only out of compassion, have considered supporting her in dealing with this misfortune, using it as an opportunity to learn in order to prevent something like this from happening again.

Sally realised that by nurturing this ridiculous notion she was even more naive than she had previously allowed herself to believe.

The trade in the shares of United Pedals did, in due course, give rise to scrutiny – as would any transaction taking place just before an acquisition of publicly-traded stock. All hope of tracing the beneficiaries of the trade would, after protracted enquiry, be abandoned, but there was an investigation by the Financial Conduct Authority into whether there had been a leak of price-sensitive information by insiders which caused much consternation and embarrassment to the firm.

Sally received nothing from MacAmbroses (not even for the last month she had worked there) since she was in serious breach of her contract.

Her stripping bare was complete. She knew that there could be no way back from her deep personal humiliation.

17.

RETREAT

As soon as Sally had managed to limp back to the flat later that evening, she phoned her mother. They had been talking to each other once a week in what had now become a closer relationship.

"Sally? Is that you? Is anything the matter?"

Sally smiled to herself because a true and proper answer would have required the dimensions of a telephone book – not a telephone call.

Is anything the matter? Well, everything was the matter! On this one day, the man she loved had left her – for what, for whom, and why?

Is anything the matter? On this one day, she had realised that she had been royally duped, taken in by a man who had shown no interest in her but only in making money – and making it dishonestly.

Is **anything the matter?** On this one day, whatever self-respect she had maintained had now been abstracted from her.

Is anything the matter? On this one day, she had lost her home.

Is anything the matter? On this one day, she had lost her job and any chance of getting a similar one.

Is anything the matter? On this one day, by dint of unthinkingly disclosing just one simple word, she had squandered over four years of study and the opportunity to join her chosen profession.

Is anything the matter? On this one day, she had been humiliated by a man who had previously had a high opinion of her.

Is anything the matter? On this one day, the full realisation had dawned on her that she had no friends.

Is anything the matter? On this one day, she had cried more than she had ever cried before.

"Nothing's the matter Ma, but I would like to come home to stay for a bit. Is that OK with you?"

"Of course, darling. When were you thinking of coming?"

"Tonight."

"Tonight? Gosh, that's wonderful. What time?"

"I'll be late, so don't wait up for me. Just leave the back door off the latch."

Sally scurried through each room gathering up in a small case those few things she needed. She ignored the mess in the kitchen (other than one £50 note which she needed for the fare to Manchester) and was pleased to find her black notebook which had been lying on the floor in the bedroom. Sally slammed the front door as loudly as she could and got a taxi to Euston, where she was fortunate to catch a train leaving in the next twenty minutes for Manchester Piccadilly. She boarded immediately and settled down to sleep.

When she awoke, Sally felt she had been sleeping for hours. However, she saw that the train had not yet left Euston. It was a 70-year-old woman (give or take a few years) who had disturbed her.

"Would you be able to look after my suitcase, please, while I fetch a cup of tea?" the woman asked.

*"… Can I get **you** one at the same time?"*

Sally was still in sleep mode and simply said *'yes'*, when what she really meant was *'Please leave me alone or I will throw myself out of the train as soon as it leaves Euston.'*

By the time the woman had returned with the two teas, the train was travelling at pace – and so was their conversation. How Sally had established such a rapport so quickly with Rosemary when all they had in common was Manchester was hard for Sally to understand especially since she had been in no mood to converse with anyone. Perhaps, she thought, they were two lonely souls who could not bear the prospect of three hours of silence – although that is what Sally had craved. Perhaps it was just one of those rare magical occasions when strangers instinctively realise that they have met a kindred spirit.

Sally knew a bit about what makes a good listener and was aware that few people have the necessary suite of skills to excel in that endeavour. A good listener needs to be patient and to avoid interrupting despite a natural urge to do so. That urge is difficult to resist since it requires a memory good enough to enable us to *'copy and save'* the proposed intervention so as to be able to *'paste'* it, later on, in the conversation. Good listeners must also resist the inclination to relate what they are being told to themselves because that will distract them from the need to concentrate on the person they are supposed to be listening to.

Sally unloaded to Rosemary everything that had happened to her the previous day, which required her to trust a stranger, however, it was exactly because Rosemary **was** a stranger (but one who showed such empathy and understanding) that Sally had been able to open her soul.

The more Rosemary quietly listened, the more abundant were Sally's tears. Somehow Rosemary reacted as if she were an experienced bereavement counsellor. Had the journey been longer, Sally would have outpoured even more, but when she began to talk about her grandmother, Rosemary leant forward and gently placed her hand on her arm – they were arriving at Manchester Piccadilly.

Sally realised that she had monopolised the whole conversation and had asked nothing about Rosemary. Sally apologised.

Sally helped Rosemary to retrieve her suitcase and they promised each other they would keep in touch.

Rosemary had enjoyed her journey and Sally had been transformed by hers.

Talking with Rosemary had been a thoroughly cathartic experience for Sally – and all on this one day. She felt a calmness and a determination to rise out of the enormous mess which was her life, which meant that, when she eventually got home to Ashton-under-Lyne that night to find her mother waiting for her, she was able to greet her without falling into a swamp of self-pity.

Sally was comfortable being back home in the cocoon of her small childhood bedroom – formerly the beloved retreat of Alice as well. She felt safe there – absorbed as she was in her duvet and her thoughts.

On countless occasions over the next few weeks she played over in her mind all that she had been through; on each play-through something new occurred to her – sometimes a realisation of the real significance of something small Tony had said to her; sometimes a recollection of relevant events she had forgotten. She berated herself a lot and was perpetually consumed with thoughts of what might have been had she not been so stupid. Try as she might, she could not think of anything else.

She could not forgive herself for that act of stupidity. What aggravated her state of anguish even more was the awareness that it was merely the careless articulation of just one word consisting of two syllables and six letters that had caused such a seismic upheaval in her life.

She was also suffering from the constant ordeal of having to deal with the regulatory authorities and without any prospect of being able to challenge them in any way. They did not, could not, would not take into account that what they were dealing with was simply the consequence of an innocent girl's foolishness. She longed for some sympathy, some understanding to accompany the strict regime of compliance; but she knew that she was dealing with the Financial Conduct Authority – not the Friendly Confession Authority.

The regular flow of correspondence between them was not only tedious for Sally but a constant reminder of her own failure and she fell into an even deeper depressed state.

Sally persevered in dealing with the FCA but was certain that she was making a lot of mistakes in handling the situation. However, she had acknowledged that any prospect of a life in the law was definitely over, so there was no point in putting much effort into dealing with the daily toil of letters or in getting legal advice – particularly since she had no money to pay for it.

The fact that, at the first opportunity, Sally had admitted her involvement in the disclosure of information had counted well for her, and she was eventually informed that there would be no proceedings brought against her by the FCA.

As regards her standing as a trainee solicitor, Sally would have to contend with another three-letter acronym – SRA – the Solicitors Regulation Authority. A full report had been sent by MacAmbroses to the SRA and as a result she was formally barred from taking any future traineeship to become a solicitor.

She could not bring herself to look for a new job. The very thought of that prospect made her shudder. What work could she turn to which would not remind her continually that she was meant for something better, something more demanding or more rewarding which would enable her to show off her true skills?

She had spoken with her mother about this, but Sally did not feel confident that her mother had fully understood the ramifications. It was as if her mother was merely going through the motions of being a loving mother. She certainly did not make herself an informed adviser, although she was, in the main, a comforting shoulder for Sally to cry on.

Sally spent most of her time in her room at home bemoaning what she had lost. She thought of Alice but could not bring herself to call her because that would have involved spelling out the litany of disastrous decisions that she had made.

She also came to think of Rosemary and recollected just how elevating their encounter on that train journey two months earlier had been. This prompted Sally, one morning, to call her; she had indeed promised to call, but it took Sally a further week to get round to charging her dead cell phone.

She questioned what the point might be of her, a 25-year-old 'depressee' who hardly left her room, starting up a friendship with a woman who was at least forty years her senior. She would be much better off, she told herself, using her time to make friends with someone nearer her age who might have more in common with her. But there was good reason for Sally to make contact – she credited her meeting with Rosemary on the train that awful day as having saved her life. As Sally's phone was coming back to life, so was her eagerness to talk to Rosemary.

In the upshot, Rosemary was delighted that Sally had called her. They met for tea and cakes and the combination of Rosemary's common sense and the sugar rush went a long way to help Sally's recovery.

Sally made sure she kept quiet on this occasion; it was Rosemary's opportunity to talk. She told Sally that she, too, was a twin and that her biggest regret had been falling out with her twin brother. They had argued over a nonsensical difference of opinion concerning some family photographs and there had been a period of more than three years during which they had not spoken to each other. Rosemary had been unable to bring herself to look at those photos again and had destroyed them.

This led to Sally mentioning Alice and to Rosemary's suggestion (so gently made) that Sally should contact her.

Rosemary's words had hit home, and Sally did indeed call Alice in Cumbria later that day. Alice took so long to answer that Sally had been about to put the phone down.

It was clear that Alice knew nothing of Sally's problems – at least Alice never referred to them. She sounded aloof and cold towards Sally and it soon became clear why. She had separated from Yusef two months previously, following the closure of some business they had set up together. Sally had sufficient empathy to be able to say all the right things to Alice and within minutes the sisters were talking together as if they had last spoken the day before yesterday. They even laughed the first proper laugh either of them had enjoyed for ages and it was the more significant for being shared.

One conversation led to another and Alice persuaded Sally to visit her in Lowca. It could have gone in the other direction, but the promise of the sea air decided it.

The next day Sally made her way via several buses to see her estranged sister. Sally was bored on the first of these and, despite the company of two books and the *Manchester Evening News*, found herself glancing around in the hope that Rosemary might, by some faint chance, also be on the bus.

Sally and Alice walked and talked for three days without intermission, so thrilled were they, once again, to be in each other's company.

Sally felt comfortable enough to be able to disclose to Alice how her denouement had occurred – how her traineeship and her projected career in the law had come to such an abrupt end. Sally included all the unsavoury details other, that is, than the MI5 element.

Alice was taken aback and demonstrably upset – not only because Sally's intense work and her dreams were now spent but because she had not been part of Sally's life at a time when she had needed her the most.

The twins were, perhaps unknowingly, treating Sally's visit to Lowca as an experiment for bigger things, and, indeed, it did not take them long to decide 'to run away together' on a trip around Europe. They chuckled about that and made plans to go off the following month for an indeterminate holiday. They told each other that they both deserved it, and they delighted in the serendipity of both being available to engage in such an adventure.

Alice decided that if they did go travelling together it would only be fair if their first port of call was Quimper.

18.
EUROPEAN TRAVEL

Alice's backpacking trip in Europe had been some years earlier, but, nevertheless, it provided her with sufficient confidence to be able to plan where they would be going after Quimper. Money was their biggest problem and they decided that they would have to rely heavily on youth hostels.

That decision was followed by a most unexpected, but timely, happening and one which they took as a harbinger of a successful foreign trip for them.

One morning at breakfast, after Sally had returned to Ashton-under-Lyne from her visit to Lowca, she was opening another unwelcome official-looking brown envelope which she had left lying around on the kitchen table for the past few days. She held the milk jug in one hand and a letter in the other, distractedly overfilling her cereal bowl as a consequence of the completely unexpected contents:

Dear Miss Bridge,

Having now exhausted our enquiries, we enclose in your favour a cheque for £4,850, being the cash found at your home last May, to which it has been decided you have the best claim.

Yours etc.

After the recent barrage of unwelcome brown envelopes, this was a missive from heaven. Sally, nevertheless, entertained a nagging doubt about whether she should keep this money. Three things served to counter such hesitation – first, Sally had now received this gift twice and she took this occasion as a sign. Next, it had come to her not from Tony but from the regulatory authorities so that it could not be treated as coming from him. Finally, the money would make all the difference between a successful holiday around Europe and a mediocre one.

Sally called Alice to tell her about the windfall and she screamed with excitement. In the space of a week the humour of both twins had improved beyond recognition.

"Who would believe," Sally asked, *"that this'll be the first time I will have stepped foot outside these shores? I can't tell you how excited I am. Do you think we should plan our route or should we just leave it to chance?"*

"Just leave all that to me. I will be in charge of the itinerary if you will look after our finances."

Alice acknowledged in all this that Sally would have the more difficult task since she would have to make decisions on their outgoings without any idea of how long they might be 'on the road'.

And that was the extent of their forward planning; barring, that is, one further bit of housekeeping. They agreed between themselves in advance that their priority would always be to look out for each other and, as far as possible, not to let the other out of sight.

A month later, they ferried and bussed to Quimper and from there made their way to Paris where they found that their mantra would be difficult to put into practice no matter how many times they might voice it. It did not make much sense for both of them to visit this or that museum if the other preferred to go to that or this art gallery and so they often spent little time with each other during the day. This had the advantage that they were less likely to be bored with each other's company at night. Moreover, by separating, they could between them visit twice as many places of interest.

They managed to hitch a lift to Amsterdam from one of the organists of the Westerkerk, a large Protestant church in the centre of Amsterdam, in which Rembrandt was buried and which they later visited together.

Alice did not feel brave enough to share with Sally the details of her relationship with Yusef until they had reached Belgium. They stayed for two weeks in a charming Relais close to a forest situated in the south of the city of Spa. It would be their first sojourn outside a city centre and the ideal setting to enable them to unwind and discard the paraphernalia of metropolitan living. From their Relais they could walk for hours in any direction and be in harmony with everything nature had to offer, all in splendid silence but for the sound of running water from the many springs and waterfalls.

On one of their idyllic walks in the forest, Alice, prompted by the setting, interrupted the silence and began to open up slowly and deliberately about her and Yusef.

She told Sally that their decision to take up her gesture and live in the house in Lowca had been accompanied by an agreement to try to set up some business together in Whitehaven although they had had no idea what.

"Neither of us had any experience that could steer us in the direction of any particular trade ... we spent hours together thumbing trade directories, reading local newspapers ... walking the streets of Whitehaven, all in an effort to find some inspiration."

Alice divulged that they had considered setting up a carpet cleaning service, since they had thought it would not involve much outlay over and above the renting of a van and cleaning apparatus, but there appeared to be too much competition.

They had also contemplated setting up as pest control specialists.

"But I'm still afraid of wasps and so is Yusef."

Window cleaning, she said, was another possibility, but due to her fear of heights, that too had been discarded as it had been agreed that any business venture had to be one in which they could work together as a team.

In desperation, they had changed tack once again and thought about what Whitehaven might expect from a new business run by the two of them.

"Being Turkish, Yusef thought that they could have expected him to provide Turkish coffee, drums or rugs … or maybe Turkish delight and baklava!"

Alice continued her account to Sally.

"We didn't want to get busy with importing stuff, so we examined opening a kebab shop, even though that didn't seem to be practical, since taking a lease would have been much too heavy a commitment. So we'd run out of ideas. However, just a few days later, I happened to read a newspaper article about concessions in shops, and it occurred to me that we could perhaps set up a kebab concession, say, in a fish and chip shop. We agreed to give it a go and visited all the chippies of Whitehaven, buying a portion of chips from each of them and looking to see whether any had a big enough corner in which to house a kebab counter. It was on the off-chance because even if we could find an ideal site in any particular shop, the owner might not be interested."

Sally did not say anything.

"Hey … are you even listening, Sally?"

"Yes, do go on. I'm quiet only because I'm fascinated."

Sally might also have been quiet as a result of contemplating why her sister had not consulted her on any of this. Sally might not know anything about fish and chip shops or kebabs, but she did have a little of the kind of knowledge which might have been helpful to Alice and Yusef in their quest. The truth was that it had crossed Alice's mind to talk to Sally but to have done so would have been to recognise her own inadequacies when Alice was still infinitely confident in her own counsel and decision-making abilities.

"We did happen to find an ideal site and Yusef did a great selling-job, persuading the owner that by providing a choice of food to their customers they would increase footfall. To cut a long story short, the owner went for it, and within six months me and Yusef were up and running. It was well-received and the business started to build up to a point where we were expecting we'd soon be in profit – a small one, but that didn't matter. We were beginning to have high hopes. However, within … it was about two months late … we had to close down for reasons completely outside our control – the chippy was

*shut down by the Cumbria hygiene people for lack of cleanliness in the kitchen, even though **our** counter was completely fine. So we too had to close completely and we lost everything."*

There was silence while Alice allowed Sally to take in the enormity of what had happened.

"Well, Yusef couldn't take it and he immediately began to drink – to drink a lot. What I didn't know was that he'd been an alcoholic. I couldn't help him, although I did try so very hard, telling him that we could manage a set-back like this, but he just went from bad to worse. He told me that he was homesick and hated Whitehaven, hated England, and I suppose this was his goodbye message because I have not seen him since. I think he was too embarrassed to face me or even himself; he was so ashamed that he had failed again, so completely and so quickly. He didn't have any appetite to try anything else. He called me from Dover, crying and saying that his mind was made up and that he was so sorry."

*"That's what Tony told **me**, but he never called me – from anywhere!"*

❖ ❖ ❖

Their meanderings took them to Frankfurt, Terplice and then to Prague where one evening when the twins were exploring the city, they briefly

186

wandered apart. Alice was looking for a postcard of the Male Namesti Fountain, while Sally was examining the fountain itself, at a distance of no more than fifty metres or so.

Sally looked up when she heard someone scream her name and saw, sprinting towards her, a determined young male clutching a bum-bag. Sally knew that it was Alice's because they had bought identical bags to hold their money, credit card and passport. The young man was running straight towards her and it stupidly occurred to her that he might now also be after **her** bum-bag. There was no time to think further and as he came level with her in the street, she stuck out her foot and tripped him up. It seemed to Sally that he had hurt himself badly, however, she did not wait to find out. After checking that Alice was none the worse and that all the contents of the bum-bag were there, she quickly led her by the arm to somewhere safe. They found a bar nearby, where they were able to have a drink, lick their wounds and reflect on what had just happened.

"I'd taken off my bum-bag to pay for a couple of postcards when that thug grabbed my bum-bag, pushed me to the ground and ran off. All I could think to do was

scream your name … Actually, I didn't even think about it. Calling you was an instinctive reaction."

Alice took a big mouthful of her hot chocolate as if it were a tot of gin. She needed both.

"Are you OK? Were you hurt at all?" Sally enquired.

"No, no, I'm fine, I'm fine. But what about you?"

"Well you know that I did some Krav Maga at uni and that I've never previously had the opportunity to use it …"

" … No way! You didn't attack him, did you?"

*"… I just tripped him up, but in any event, we are now quits. You got me **my** passport – and now I have got you **yours**!"* and they both laughed.

They then went on to Vienna and from there took a train to Italy, visiting Venice, Verona, Trento, Florence, Naples and Rome.

When they got to Italy Sally and Alice decided they would look for work waiting on tables in restaurants so as to afford themselves a little more luxury and an extension of their grand tour. They found separate jobs in both Verona and Florence but worked together in Naples although not at the same time. The vacancy they found in Naples was at a pizzeria looking for someone to work six days a week. With their hair then being the same length, it was possible for the girls to work three days each, with Sally covering for Alice and Alice for Sally so as to give each of them time to enjoy the city. They did not believe that the proprietor suspected that the girls were job-sharing until, on their last day, Sally was presented with a wink and double pay for the day.

Neither of the girls had expected their extended journeying together to be as harmonious as it was turning out to be. They had reached Barcelona and had hardly had any quarrels or misunderstandings other than a few inconsequential differences. The trip also meant that all recriminations between them were forgotten. What might have been a journey of arguments turned out to be warm and relaxed because of Sally having subcontracted to Alice all decisions concerning the route. It was a most effective algorithm, enabling them to talk more easily about the things that mattered.

Sally had even felt comfortable enough to tell Alice of her involvement with the security services from whom she had received no communication for over four years. That indicated either that they did not care or that they did not even know of her existence. Either way, she felt free to tell her sister, who then had a hundred and one questions, none of which Sally could properly answer either to Alice's satisfaction or her own.

They both looked relaxed as they sat in the afternoon sun drinking coffee in one of the many bars and restaurants along Las Ramblas. It was '*postcard sending time*', and both Sally and Alice were hard at it. Sally always took a long time on her postcards. As there was little space in which to write, Sally took it slowly even though the price of an error was merely the cost of a new postcard. She really thought about what she wanted to say and whether there would be enough room on the card in which to say it.

In contrast, Alice machine-gunned the things she had to say without any prior thought and without considering what space there was.

"Who are you sending those two postcards to?" she asked Sally.

*"I'm writing to Rosemary. You remember – she's the woman who kept me together on the journey back from London. I've been writing to her quite a bit since we left Oldham ... the other is to Ben Ashcrofte from MacAmbroses. He is the only person from there I still keep in touch with ... who are **you** writing to?"*

"I'm writing to Jose, but I'm not sure it's such a good idea, having not been in touch with him for such a long time. I thought that when we get to Madrid he might show us around, but I'm having second thoughts. He might not be living in Madrid now anyway and he is probably married with five kids."

And with that she took hold of the postcard and tore it into small shreds, working with such intensity and purpose that Sally thought that it was as if Alice was seeking to destroy not only the postcard but also any lingering regrets she might have had on breaking up with Jose.

"Anyway," Alice added as an afterthought, *"we are much better relying on our own company."*

Sally decided that it would be imprudent to question Alice about her relationship with Jose and decided to talk instead about another relationship.

"Do you think that's why we've never been able to create a strong bond with Ma, you know, the kind of connection which most daughters and mothers would expect to enjoy between them?"

*"Maybe … as much as I love her, I must admit that she is a bit of a weirdo. She has always encouraged the two of us to commune together rather than make any real effort to establish any close connection with **her**. It's as if*

she has always been pleased to let us get on with it or even glad to push us away. I can't really understand it."

"*I know what you mean, Alice. You remember the arrangement we had as kids where you would handle Pa and I'd deal with Ma; well, I can assure you that there was nothing which enabled me to get closer to Ma than you could.*"

"*Perhaps it's our fault. Maybe we edged her out.*"

"*I don't think that's of our doing. Ma is happy with the way things have always been. In the same way as we are happy in our own company, so are Ma and Pa. It suits them.*"

They paused for thought, looked at each other and both began writing postcards to Ma.

19.
MR CHAMBERS

After a week in Barcelona, they visited Tarragona, Zaragoza, Madrid and then Toledo.

Their next port of call was Lisbon, where they arrived after 14 months of sightseeing ready to carry out yet another exhaustive city exploration. Their plan was then to go to Porto where they would decide whether (and, if so, how) they would make their way home to England, the speed of travel depending on how much would then remain in the joint purse.

Apart from making a few telephone calls home, sending some postcards and collecting two *poste restante* packages from Ma (one in Naples and one in Vienna) Sally and Alice had not been in contact with anyone from home and they had been able to forget their woes.

For them both to have forgotten about life back home (and, in particular, the need to work on their future career paths) might have appeared to any fellow traveller to be somewhat indulgent or even reckless.

They had expected real life eventually to catch up with them, and, indeed, it did when they reached Lisbon, their third planned *poste restante*, where a letter from England was awaiting them.

While Alice was still asleep, Sally had sauntered down to the *agência dos Correios*. They had agreed three *postes restante* with Ma just in case there might be something she needed to send them when they were away. As she was congratulating herself on how well the system appeared to be working, Sally was handed an envelope from England addressed, unusually, to the both of them. Instead of waiting for Alice, Sally allowed impatience to get the better of her and began to open it.

The letter was from a solicitor informing Alice and Sally of the deaths of both of their parents on 5 August.

Sally received the news as a boxer would receive a clean, heavy blow direct to the head. She was overwhelmed and unsteady on her feet; she had to sit down in the square before she could read on or do anything else. They had last spoken to their mother some ten days ago.

Sally's first thought, which stayed with her for some time, was that she had not said *'goodbye'*. That such sentiment should be her first reaction to the news was a further surprise for Sally.

When she calmed down, she realised that she did not feel the deep sense of grief and emptiness she would have expected to feel. Maybe, she thought, that would come in time. She hoped so because she was beginning to experience a profound sense of guilt – guilt that she was not distraught as a result of the sudden loss of both of her parents. Surely that was unnatural; am I really such an unfeeling bitch, she kept on asking herself. Her mind raced from self-hating to self-protecting thoughts in an effort to answer her own question. No! It was not that she was unfeeling or unloving. It was that the bond between her and her parents had broken a long time ago and it was then that she had done her real mourning.

The solicitor explained in his letter that he had been appointed the sole executor of the Wills of Mr G Bridge and Mrs S Bridge and he conveyed his condolences. The letter went on to suggest that the girls return home as soon as possible as the Bridges had left the whole of their estate to be shared equally between Alice and Sally.

The letter contained a lot of information for Sally to absorb but omitted much else that she wanted to know. She had an overriding need, first, to ascertain how her parents had died and an urge (which bizarrely was almost as strong) to find out her parents' full names. What 27-year-olds do not know the names of their parents?

She looked again at the letter. How was it that she could have arrived at a point where she did not know how her parents had died and, even worse, how they had lived?

She returned quickly to show the letter to Alice, who was shaken by it to a much greater extent than Sally had been. It took an hour, a shower and two cups of coffee before Alice could talk coherently to Sally.

They read the letter together again and immediately booked tickets for a flight leaving Lisbon for Manchester late that night. Their trip abroad had lasted exactly 14 months. Yes! – it **had** been a self-indulgent adventure – **that**, the girls admitted to each other – but they were also able to persuade each other that they had been in dire need of it and that they had deserved it.

The two of them hardly spoke to each other on the flight home, so lost were they in their own thoughts. They each read the letter again several times on the plane, examining both the envelope and the letter carefully as if there might be some sign of a hoax, since neither of them could believe that two healthy adults could die at such an early age.

An hour into the flight, they began to talk to each other again. Had there been a car accident? Or some other accident? Had they been murdered? That was less fanciful an explanation than their parents having committed suicide, which they did not even contemplate.

Once they had landed, they decided they did not want to go to their parents' home before speaking to the solicitor, a Mr G F S L Chambers LLB. They tried calling his number at frequent intervals from 8.30am until a receptionist answered and put Alice through. All the time, Sally was leaning her head towards Alice's, straining to hear what Mr Chambers had to say. Alice asked whether they could meet him that morning, explaining that they had just returned from an extended holiday and were waiting in a café nearby. Mr Chambers apologised, saying that he could only spare them half an hour. Alice was on the point of asking Mr Chambers how their parents had died when she decided that this was best done in person.

Mr Chambers' offices were well-trodden and cramped, but a warm and welcoming room awaited them. Mr Chambers was affable and he immediately made Alice and Sally feel at ease despite the circumstances of their visit. Notwithstanding a long career in the profession, he did not appear to be infused with the kind of unctuousness that funeral parlour directors often exude as a result of so frequently having to offer their condolences and to immerse themselves in the grief of others.

Although the girls had arranged the meeting to find out how their parents had died, Mr Chambers began by explaining the effect of the Bridges' Wills.

Mr Chambers advised them that they would each be entitled to half the value of their parents' joint estate, consisting of their semi-detached home in Ashton-under-Lyne and a bank account with nearly £53,000 in it. There would be no inheritance tax, but there would be expenses and the mortgage to repay. He estimated that, in time, after the sale of the house, each of the daughters would receive a distribution of roughly £100,000 from the estate, but that depended on what price they would get on the sale of the house.

Mr Chambers asked Sally and Alice whether either or both of them might want to live in the family home or whether it should be sold; but they both replied, looking at each other questioningly, that it was far too early for them to make any decisions of that sort. Unknown to the other, they both harboured a desire that, after their resoundingly successful experiment on the continent (despite its calamitous ending) they might, indeed, want to live with each other. They both diarised in their memory banks the need to discuss this unexpected possibility with each other at the first opportunity.

The Wills also contained two rather curious bequests – a gift of 'The Green Box and its contents' to Sally and a gift of 'The Blue box and its contents' to Alice. The bequests were curious because neither Mr Chambers nor the twins had any idea what these boxes were, where they could be found or

what might be in them. But Mr Chambers still had a
lot of clearing out to do.

The administration of their parents' estate, he
said, was unlikely to give rise to much
complication, but there was still the Coroner's
hearing and the funerals to come. He estimated that
obtaining probate and selling the house would take
a few months and that the final distributions would
be in about a year's time.

Sally asked Mr Chambers whether he had met
their parents. He replied that he had seen them
twice. He would not have taken instructions for a
Will, he said, without face-to-face contact and
obtaining full details of their affairs. Sally thought
that that must have been an intrusive experience for
both her parents.

"How did they seem?" asked Sally.

"Well," Mr Chambers replied without any
degree of pomposity, *"there is a limit to what I can tell
you. It was Mr and Mrs Bridge who were my clients and
I have a duty of confidentiality. Many apologies; I have
to leave."*

And with that he was gone. A young lad, called
Cedric, came into Mr Chamber's office, introduced

himself and said that he had been asked to show them out.

Mr Chambers had still not got round to explaining how their parents had died. He had been in a hurry; he had talked too quickly and the girls had found it difficult to interrupt him. It was if Mr Chambers was trying to avoid the question although they knew that he could hardly be party to any conspiracy to withhold such information from them.

20.

THE CORONER

Not much of what Sally's mother had explained to her on Sally's 14th birthday turned out to be accurate.

To start with, her parents were not married and never had been. Marriage would have involved divulging their names, in addition to having to deal with all the other paraphernalia and formalities of getting married.

They had not gone to Turkey on holiday – they had fled from their respective parents.

Their names in their passports were Sylvia Imber and George Bridge.

Their mother had not been able to summon the strength or the courage to tell her parents: (a) that she would not be finishing her degree course (b) that she was pregnant (c) that she was expecting twins (d) that she was not proposing to marry the father (e) who was German and (f), incidentally, that they were both escaping to Turkey – perhaps forever.

Such was her familiarity with the prejudices of her parents and their strict moral code that Sylvia knew that giving them that information, or even any part of it, would have destroyed them.

Their father had been equally as cowardly. He was no more able to go to Düsseldorf to explain his plans to his family than Sylvia was able to reveal the truth to **her** family. There was no big debate. The couple knew what they had to do and what they could not possibly do.

All of this information had come out, bit by bit, bite by bite, on the day of the Coroner's hearing at *Manchester South Coroner's Court,* called to look into their parents' suicides. Sally and Alice listened transfixed throughout.

There were many further intensely personal items of information about their parents that emerged that day in open court, each of which, when they were disclosed, barb by barb, blow by blow, proved the more hurtful to Sally and Alice by reason of having been withheld from them.

- Their parents had met at Manchester University in 1984 on the first day of their four-year degree course in French and Spanish. They had hardly left each other's side while they were at university, and they had made few, if any, other friends.
- They had gone to Turkey in 1987, when Sylvia was three months' pregnant.
- Neither of them had graduated.
- Both of Sylvia's parents, Max and Julia Imber, were Jewish. Sylvia's father was born in Radom, Poland in 1925 and her mother in London in 1928. Her mother had gone to live in Brussels with her parents and three brothers in 1933, when she was seven years old.
- Sylvia's parents were both survivors of concentration camps – her mother had survived Auschwitz Birkenau and her father had been an inmate of Majdanek.
- All of her mother's family, including her mother's parents and their three sons, had perished in Auschwitz Birkenau.

- All of her father's family, including her father's parents and their six children, had perished in Majdanek.

- Sylvia's parents had met in an army hospital in 1945. They had married in 1946 and found their way, in the same year, to Whitehaven, where there was a need for Max Imber's experience in chemistry.

- Sylvia's parents had tried to suppress the trauma they had endured during the Holocaust, but they nevertheless continued to suffer untold mental torment and psychological problems, leaving them, for the remainder of their lives, with a despair often described as *'survivor syndrome'*.

- Sylvia Imber lived with her parents in Cumbria for 24 years. Her father had died in Cumbria in 1985 and her mother in Ashton-under-Lyne in 1997.

- There was evidence from a doctor that Sylvia Imber had, throughout her life, been deeply affected by the accounts she had heard of the suffering of her parents and their families. He had written that *'... the mental health of Sylvia Imber was so serious that in comparing her state of health with that of her mother it was not easy to differentiate between survivor and second generation'*. He went on to say that the pain, sorrow and guilt suffered by Mr and Mrs Imber had permeated, in no small dose, down to their daughter, Sylvia. It had been her escape to Manchester University which had saved her from a complete breakdown.

- Sylvia's parents had conceived great plans for her, but she had consistently fallen below what had been expected of her as a young girl and this had made Sylvia feel guilty and disenchanted with her life.

- When Sylvia first mentioned to her parents that George Bridge was originally called 'Jorg Günter Brücke' they had become disorientated.

- Jorg Brücke was born in Düsseldorf and had changed his name in 1974 to George Bridge. He, too, had been sorely affected by the Holocaust and, in particular, by what his parents had told him about his father's brother being involved in Kemna concentration camp. George had always suffered intense guilt about that. So ruthless had the torture of prisoners been in Kemna that the Nazis had felt obliged to close the camp in 1934 only six months after it had been opened for fear that public opinion would turn against them.

- Sylvia Imber and George Bridge had chosen to go to Turkey in 1987. George Bridge had a cousin there and an offer of employment but they were not able to settle there.
- Sylvia Imber had no cousins in Swansea. Indeed, she had no family other than George Bridge and their two daughters.
- When Mr Chambers was preparing their Wills, he was given no indication of the mental state of either George Bridge or Sylvia Imber and he certainly had no idea of any plan they might have had to engage in a suicide pact.
- They had committed suicide by sedating themselves and putting their heads into the gas oven in their kitchen in Ashton-under-Lyne.

On the receipt of this last piece of information, Sally and Alice broke down, and the Court had to adjourn.

The two of them stayed in their seats crying and holding on to each other; gripping each other's clothes in despair and bewilderment. There was no one to comfort them but each other.

There was no saying how much pain they were feeling as they realised that they were not who they thought they were. Their parents had together made the decision that they would live a lie. The twins had gone to sleep the one day and woken up the next in a new reality, with a new identity. Disclosure by disclosure, layer by layer, Sally and Alice's very essence had been stripped bare; the shock of such loss of selfhood being compounded by grief for their parents.

The Coroner resumed the proceedings after an hour and his conclusion was that George Bridge had taken his own life while the balance of his mind was disturbed. There was the same verdict for Sylvia Imber.

The funeral took place at Dukinfield Crematorium & Cemetery four days later.

Mr Chambers attended the funeral.

Only nine mourners were present.

As they walked away from their parents' graves, Sally and Alice thanked Mr Chambers for being there. With his head bowed, unable to face the twins, unable to find anything meaningful to say to them, he merely expressed his condolences under his breath.

Sally and Alice got a taxi to the house; **they** could not face **anyone**.

When they stepped inside, they found two envelopes on the doormat, each marked 'NOT TO

BE OPENED UNTIL AFTER OUR FUNERALS' and addressed 'To Alice and Sally'. How they got there they could only guess.

Sally and Alice were bewildered. Could there be yet further secrets to be revealed? What more could there possibly be to torment them?

They held back from opening the letters until they had settled down next to each other, shoulder to shoulder, on Sally's bed in their old bedroom. Thank God they had each other.

The letters were in their mother's hand, written with a fountain pen in blue ink:

4th August 2014

Dear Alice and Sally,

Pa and I apologise for being abysmal parents. We both love you very much and stress that you must not feel responsible in the minutest way for our decision.

You will be looking for some explanation, but there is too much to say, and having not said enough to you while I was with you, I cannot now bring myself to give you anything other than the briefest account of what I feel. It is not meant to burden you but to help you, if at all possible, to understand just a little of our malaise.

I made a mess of my childhood. It was not a good time for me. I was constantly unhappy and didn't have a sister or brother to share things with. I somehow couldn't make or couldn't keep friends. That was how it was - however unnatural. I have always regretted not getting the best out of my education and not graduating. The _only_ good thing was meeting Pa.

I suppose that I was deeply affected by your grandparents' account of the camps and that is why (and I regret it so much) I kept my distance from you so as to keep you from being affected in the way that I was. But I went much too far. I know that I should have told you that you are Jewish and given you the opportunity to grow up as Jews.

We felt impelled to protect you by not telling you. We had the notion that if the two of you didn't know you were Jewish, then no one else would. We behaved like young kids playing hide and seek, believing that if we were being hunted we would remain invisible merely by closing our eyes.

I realise how unnatural I have been and I regret not talking to you, embracing you, teaching you and doing all the countless things that any normal mother would do.

We feel so inadequate as parents because not only have we been distant but we have also been secretive to the point of madness. Yes, 'madness' is probably what it is. We were secretive of who we are, and we have denied you the opportunity to learn about your heritage. To make things even worse, I have also let down my parents, who never abandoned the notion of an Imber dynasty.

In trying to avoid doing to you what my parents did to me, I have perhaps created even more problems, but your Pa and I know that you are two wonderful human beings with a resilience which will bring you through anything.

We are so proud that despite our making such a mess of our responsibility to you, you are so loving and supportive of each other, *and we are certain that you will both shine and be happy.*

Your Ma and Pa feel so guilty about all our stupid errors regarding Sally's birth certificate. We know the anxiety it caused was only partly alleviated by the actions of Alice, to whom we are so grateful for what she achieved in putting things right.

My darlings, do what you can and be happy.

Finally, this letter is not meant as an explanation of what we have done, because my mind has been in such turmoil that I am not sure of anything. All I know is that both Pa and I feel it is the only way for us to halt the overpowering pain of failure.

It was signed *'Your Ma and Pa'*.

Sally registered that it was not signed *'Your loving Ma and Pa'*.

The girls compared their letters to find that they were identical. It was bizarre that in her state of anguish their mother had found the time and energy to write out an apology in long hand twice, using exactly the same words. Perhaps this was her way of showing that she had no favourite.

The fact that the apology (which is what the girls had come to call their mother's tragic letter) was cast in such definite terms made it even more painful for them to read because it emphasised the determination and resolve of their parents to end their lives. Although their mother had said she was in turmoil and unsure about things, she would not have been able to express herself in these terms unless she and their father had so conclusively, so categorically, decided to go ahead with their plans.

Sally and Alice read their tragic letters many times. They studied every word and every nuance. They talked together for hours trying to recollect any conversation with their mother which might throw light on a narrative that somehow did not make sense to either of them.

Sally and Alice discussed at length whether they might, to any extent, have contributed to their mother's suicidal impulse. They asked each other whether this would have occurred had they not gone swanning off on their trip for so many months. Should they have tried to engage more with their parents, particularly with their father?

Had they discussed these painful issues before the Coroner's hearing had taken place and before reading their mother's apology they thought that they might have accepted a large tranche of responsibility for the disastrous finale to their parents' unhappy lives. However, the apology allowed them to conclude that their parents' end would probably have been the same regardless of whether or not the twins had tried to get closer to their parents and whether or not the twins had deserted them by swanning around Europe.

The day's events had taught them much.

"Alice, as kids we had no understanding of what family life should be like. We had little ability to influence it. As adult children we now know more about what we should have expected from family life, but whatever we might have tried to do, like engaging more with Ma and Pa, they would still have rebuffed us. I can't understand it, but then perhaps we will not be able to until after we have kids of our own."

They went on to discuss their childhood and to discuss, once again, whether the closeness of their twinhood had served to '*lock out*' their parents. They could not manage to put that concern aside.

There were too many questions and too few answers.

Sally, a largely resilient and self-sufficient soul, was only now beginning to realise what she had missed in her youth. Notwithstanding her endless debates with her sister, she continued to fixate on what she might have done to enable her parents to be better parents to them. The idea that children might have an obligation to help their parents raise them seemed to Sally to be an odd notion, but if ever there was a family to whom this might have any application, then it was **her** family.

In any event, Sally felt guilt. She began, as best she could, to recall her 14th birthday and whether she should have handled matters differently. She thought about whether she had behaved badly over the Quimper trip. She pondered on so many things which she thought she should have handled better. The stream of thought was endless, and the more it continued to flow, the more she felt that guilt.

Sally's own self-protection mechanism kicked in again. She told herself that their home could not properly have been described as a *'household'*. It had been a unit only in the physical sense that the four of them slept under the same roof.

Her parents **appeared** to be happy, acting together on most family matters; and Sally and Alice had, for the most part, been a close unit. But those two units had failed to coalesce into one successful family unit.

"Perhaps few families are *'successful'*" Sally suggested to Alice.

When Sally was alone later that evening she broke down in tears yet again because she realised that she **did** feel love for her parents and that she **did** feel her loss most acutely. Sally folded the tragic letter and returned it to the privacy of its envelope, making sure it was not touched by her tears.

Although the letter was a totally one-sided discourse, Sally was sad that it was the deepest 'conversation' that she ever had with her mother.

21.
SALLY AND ALICE

After the trauma of the Coroner's hearing Sally and Alice could not bring themselves to continue to live in the family home in Ashton-under-Lyne.

They slept just one further night in the house although they could not enter the kitchen. They shuddered to think that the two of them had, the previous day, been eating breakfast there. While they were arranging to leave the house for the final time, they would use the living room.

They realised that, until they could gather themselves together, they would have to move into a hotel. Although that would be expensive they decided that there was no alternative. Perhaps as a way of sealing that decision and avoiding the temptation of going back on it, they immediately wrote to Mr Chambers and told him that neither of them wanted to live in the house and that they wanted him to arrange to sell it. They instructed Mr Chambers to dispose of the property, if necessary, at a reduced price, in order to get rid of it as quickly as possible.

They found a budget hotel in Manchester that was prepared to offer a discount if they stayed for a month. It was a twin-bedded room (aptly named, thought Sally), and they knew that they would be able to share it together successfully. They had had plenty of practice.

As they walked down the path they both glanced back at the house and its double letterboxes. Neither could bring themselves to speak; and neither of them saw Brian, next door, peering through a gap in the curtains.

Whenever anything caused either of them to recall their parents' death, they would impulsively push it back to the furthest reaches of their minds in an effort to obscure it and temporarily replace it with some other thought – **any** other thought. Perhaps this pain might have been alleviated by yet more deep conversation, but they had already talked together interminably about their feelings of guilt and they could not now take any more. Deep down, Sally suspected that to talk more with Alice on this painful subject might reveal even darker truths. She felt that her reluctance to dig further was akin to the disinclination a troubled soul might feel on being offered an appointment with a psychotherapist for fear of some unknown and unwelcome revelation. And so Sally did not broach the subject with Alice.

Neither of the twins was working and so it was natural for discussion between them to turn to what they might do to find employment. Alice would not even consider the possibility of the two of them setting up in business together. Sally had raised that prospect with Alice once before and she had, in response, uttered two dismissive words: *'Done that!'*

A constant theme as regards Alice was the possibility that she could go into a travel agency to learn the business, especially since Sally thought that she had both the talent and the experience for that line of business.

When they sat down together at mealtimes their conversations would usually turn at some point to the future. When it came to Sally's, the possibility often arose of again working in a supermarket. That was far removed from what she had originally contemplated as a career. However much she might enjoy the retail environment, she was disinclined to go back to '*shop work*'. They also talked about Sally going into retail management, which would enable her to exploit her business instincts, however, Sally did not think that she could possibly bring herself to embark on another course of study.

They had enough money to allow them to indulge in indecision for a few more months; they had no need to rush to any conclusions. Besides which, if they could manage to sell the house in Ashton-under-Lyne, they would have a useful cushion although Alice reminded Sally that probate might not be completed for many months and any pay-out would therefore be delayed. Procrastination might therefore be risky.

"Why don't we consider selling the house in Lowca as well as the house in Ashton?," Alice reflected out of nowhere one evening at supper. *"I can't see myself ever going back to live in Lowca, and we could use the proceeds to buy ourselves two new flats. What about that? I know it would mean revoking your wedding present to me, but, I'm serious … we could simply divide the total proceeds of both homes between us equally. What could be wrong with that?"*

Sally instinctively disliked the idea of taking back the *'gift'* of Lowca she had made to Alice. On principal, it did not seem right to take back any gift, however, the more she thought about it, the more sensible the plan seemed.

"It does sound like a good idea, Alice, but let's park it for the time being, if that's ok."

'Parking fees' were expensive both for the pocket and for the soul. It was uncomfortable for the girls to *'leave too many issues in the parking lot'*, so they agreed they should try to reach some concrete decisions and call a halt to their dilatoriness. They thought that this would, at least, occupy their minds and help them to get back to some kind of normality. Sally told Alice that she preferred *'normalcy'* to *'normality'* and Alice laughed, telling Sally that this was the first indication from her in many months that she might be back to her old self and, at last, moving in the right direction.

And so they played *'the decision game'*, which was a dangerous pursuit for them, seeing that it concerned something as vital as their careers. There was one rule – they would take it in turns to make a decision that each would promise to implement. Each would be put on the spot; it was like playing with dice or even a loaded revolver, and if played properly the game would have the benefit of getting them both *'off the pot'*.

It was Alice's kind of game, and she said she would go first.

She promised Sally that she would visit all the large travel agencies in Manchester and see what openings there might be for her. Although she was more than aware that job applications were normally sent by post or via email, she knew that this methodology would not suit someone as impatient as her. She would, instead, take a few hard copies of her curriculum vitae with her and seek employment using her legs rather than email.

However, when she came to think about a CV, Alice immediately became despondent, saying that she did not have anything to put in it – she had no A-levels and no degree. She did not even know anyone who could give her a reference. All she could offer was a failed venture selling kebabs in Cumbria.

"Sally, what can I possibly put in a CV to impress anyone. I'm a failure."

"That's nonsense. Travel agents are crying out for intelligent, motivated employees who have imagination and good organising skills. That describes you perfectly,

and in addition you have the ability to plan complex trips. You know that. Rather than create a traditional CV, why not prepare a short description of your experience. Have a try, and I will go through it with you."

"Thanks for the pep talk, but how can any CV I might create compare with yours with your three A stars and first-class degree?"

"Yes, but you can't stop there; go on … 'May 2013, almost prosecuted for fraud and insider dealing and disbarred forever from the legal profession'. Do you think that sounds better than yours? As soon as I mention any of my academic successes to a prospective employer, they will ask why I didn't decide to qualify or, even worse, tell me that I am overqualified for the post I'd just applied for. How do I answer that?"

And that brought Sally to **her** throw of the dice in *the decision game*. She had one minute to make her decision. She recollected what Rosemary had advised her on the train – in fact, it was the only piece of advice she had given Sally: *"When all else fails, go back to your roots."*

"Alice, I have also decided. I am going to try to get a job in Lidburys. That was probably where I have been the happiest."

And, so, by an artifice, two big decisions had been made. They fully realised that neither of them might lead anywhere, but that was not the point.

There was one other important outstanding issue occupying Sally's mind.

"As regards Lowca," she told Alice, *"I think you are quite right: I give in. I'm happy to pool the amounts we get on selling both homes and split them in half to buy two flats. I have one condition … they must be very near to each other."*

Two weeks later, Alice, who was in charge of dealing with the sale of their parents' house, received an email from Mr Chambers.

"Sally, you will never guess. We've received an offer at the asking price for the house. Mr Chambers is a star."

"Yes, the 'Star Chambers'," Sally punned, *"… he's a treasure. Even though he might not be familiar with Whitehaven, why don't you also use him to sell Lowca? I bet he'll be delighted to get an extra piece of work."*

Alice could see that Sally's appetite for wordplay and her generous spirit were continuing to return. Her depression appeared gradually to be lifting.

There was one unexpected outcome of the house being cleared for sale. *'The Star Chambers'* (as the girls now always referred to him) had asked Cedric to do the clearing and in the loft he had found two parcels which could be collected at any time from his office. The parcels, Alice found, consisted of two old dusty paper carrier bags which she took up to their hotel room so that they could open them together.

They very deliberately removed the outer wrappings and found two 1950s Huntley & Palmer biscuit tins, both of which were beginning to rust and tarnish. It was just about possible to make out their original colours – one was greenish and the other blue. These had to be the '*Green Box*' and the '*Blue Box*', referred to in their parents' Wills. Sally and Alice found it hard to open the tins; both felt this was perhaps to do with the fact that on the previous occasion they had sat on a bed together for a coordinated reading ceremony the result had been so devastating.

They could not remember whose box was whose in the Wills, but Sally took the blue box (as this was her favourite colour) and Alice the green one (that being her favourite). Their parents had not even got that right because in the Wills it was the reverse – the green box went to Sally and the blue to Alice.

So, what further revelations, they speculated, were now to confront them?

The contents were both mundane and yet extraordinary. Each box contained about twenty or so black and white photographs (with a few sepia pictures among them) but no indication as to who the subjects were. They thought that they could identify their grandparents in some of the photos almost all of which belonged to their era. There was one notable exception. At the bottom of each pile was an identical colour photo of the girls' parents which had presumably been taken while they were at university. It would be hard to find a photo showing two happier subjects. The photos shouted out: *'We have found each other! We are madly in love, and we will live forever!'*

There was something else. In each biscuit tin, they found an old small brown greaseproof paper bag containing three small candles and a matchbox full of time-worn (but live) Swan Vesta matches.

22.
LIDBURYS

Standing there in the queue on that miserably wet November evening, Sally was on the point of going home when she suddenly found that she was next. She tapped politely on Mr Leigh's door and entered his office. He glanced at her and invited her to sit down.

"Hello, my name's Sally Bridge and I am looking for a job."

Mr Leigh was obviously taken aback by Sally's bluntness.

"I see……. at present we don't actually have any vacancies. You will need to speak to the Assistant Manager, Mrs Tarkani, who will know what, if any, jobs will be coming up. I can give you her number."

"But you, Mr Leigh, are the only person I can discuss this with."

"Oh!? Why is that?"

"As I say, it's Mrs Tarkani who deals with junior job applications."

"I'm so sorry to trouble you, Mr Leigh, but the job I want to discuss with you is not a junior appointment, and it's one which only you would likely have authority to give. All I need is a few minutes to explain."

He leant forward looking puzzled. Sally had managed to capture his interest.

"I know a bit about supermarkets and believe that what's almost always missing is someone specifically designated to greet shoppers, to say goodbye to them and answer their queries. I am sure that a lot of the shoppers who come into the store feel reluctant to seek answers to their questions simply because they have to walk half-way around the store before they can get anyone to help them."

Sally paused, but he did not interrupt her and so she ventured her hand further.

"I'd see my role, if you agreed to take me on, as increasing footfall and increasing loyalty by getting to know your regular customers and establishing some kind of rapport with them. That's what I think is missing from most large stores because, even if regular customers know one or two of the checkout assistants, it's a matter of chance whether they would be served by them. I wouldn't interfere with your managers but would report to you, giving you, I'd hope, useful feedback on anything that's going on which might be of interest to you."

"Sally, that's most interesting."

And he, then, also paused.

"I'm sure the role you describe would be one which would add to our offering here, however, I know nothing about you, and we have not previously employed such front of house staff ... and, in any event, we don't have the budget for such a person ... so I'm sorry."

"I do understand, but I'm so convinced that you'd get significant results within, say, three months, and what I was going to suggest to you was that I would be prepared to work without pay for those three months so that if at the end you thought it wasn't working out, you'd simply get rid of me. I'd still come here to shop!"

Mr Leigh paused, smiled and scratched his chin with his thumb, which was perhaps as much as Sally could expect after the initial rebuff.

"Sally, as I say, your proposition is interesting. If you leave your details, I will get back to you by Friday to let you know whether Lidburys might have an opening for you. Thanks so much for coming in to see me."

Sally left the store disappointed with Mr Leigh's brusque manner. He might, she thought, have given her a little more time to talk about herself and he might have shown a bit more enthusiasm. She told herself, however, that she had given it her best shot.

Lidburys did, of course, know a great deal about Sally, and it might have helped her application if she had been able to tell Mr Leigh where to look. During her conversation with him, it occurred to Sally that she might tell him that she had spent over a year and a half working in his store as a shelf-filler some nine years previously. She stopped herself from doing so because scrutiny of Lidburys employment records would, of course, have revealed that it had been one *Alice* Bridge and not *Sally* Bridge who had worked there. She was not going to trip herself up again and she would have to content herself (and hopefully Mr Leigh) with explaining, merely, that she did have good knowledge of what went on in supermarkets.

Even if Mr Leigh had not been persuaded by her pitch, **Sally** was. She was, indeed, so persuaded and so confident of the merits of the role that she had created for herself that she decided to make appointments to see the Managers of two other local supermarkets.

Neither of them showed the slightest interest.

That was of no matter because, on the Thursday, Mr Leigh telephoned to ask her whether she would pop into the store that evening to speak to him. She was met with an entirely altered Mr Leigh. Not only did he spare her the ignominy of queueing, but this time he was welcoming and friendly and gave her as much time as she wanted. He told her that he was interested in what she had proposed to him earlier in the week, particularly since, many years ago, he had contemplated a role of the kind she had described, but it had been rejected by management because it would have been hard to make a success of the position and difficult to recruit the right people. He told Sally that she had, however, presented a compelling proposition which accommodated both of those difficulties. His human resources department had told him that Lidburys could not take on anyone to work in their stores unless they were signed up under a contract and were paid at a minimum rate, so Mr Leigh proposed a monthly salary of £1,500, a three-month trial period and a start date on Monday.

She stuck out her hand to agree, and they both laughed. *"I look forward to seeing you next week then,"* he said with a warm smile.

Mr Leigh, she thought, must have spoken to higher management at Lidburys and was told that there was little to be lost by taking Sally on in this role. Or perhaps Mr Leigh had decided to employ her on his own initiative which Sally felt would bode well. In either case, she was thrilled to have this self-made chance of a job.

Becoming a meeter and greeter in a supermarket was not what Sally had in mind when she first began her studies, but she was determined to put every effort into making a success of the opportunity. It might not suit her long-term, but for the time being, it would be the perfect job for her. Sally had a clear view of the benefits the role could bring and she had the confidence that she could deliver them.

It was some time since she had worked in the store and she knew that a lot must have changed; besides which she had only been a shelf-filler. However, she had always kept her eyes open while replenishing those shelves, and she had learned a lot. There were many things that could have been improved or done differently when she was last working in the store, but back then no one would have listened to a mere shelf-filler.

Mrs Tarkani was most helpful in getting Sally '*signed up*', as she put it. There was a minimum amount of bureaucracy – the only problem being the code which should be assigned to Sally's job. It was not even clear what Sally's title should be. Mr Leigh suggested '*Front of House*' as both the name of her position and what she should be called. He was amused by the title because it would be a reminder to him of Sally's effrontery in waltzing into his office and proposing (even insisting!) that she be appointed to a position in Lidburys which did not even exist and, what is more, which she thought **she** had created.

But he did not tell Sally any of that.

On the Monday morning, Mrs Tarkani gave Sally a two-hour induction course telling Sally that whenever she had any questions she could go to her.

Sally's role was to be a fluid one – 'sink or swim' – in that it would be left to her to devise her own procedures and job specification. For any employee, in any job, that would be a most enviable position to be in and Sally, indeed, relished it.

The same afternoon, Sally furnished herself with a small notepad, a propelling pencil and a garden chair which she placed at the side of the large newspaper stand on the right, where customers entered the store. Customers coming into the store would hardly be able to see her there concealed behind the news, but from that position **she** would be able to see a lot. She decided that that would be her eery for the next three days and she would, during that time, do nothing other than fulfil the role of an observer and the taker of copious notes.

Sally's plan was to be tireless in improving the shopping experience for the customer. She knew what customers were looking for and that the success of any store depended on excellent customer service. That could easily turn out to be a hollow mantra, she thought, unless one was canny enough to find out how to achieve such a goal. She decided that she would not pay lip service to her decision to talk to shoppers and that she would try to remember the names of the regular customers and what they told her about their lives and their in-store experience. Armed with such intelligence, greeting any customer would then mean so much more than merely bidding them an idle *'good morning!'* or an empty *'hello, how are you?'*

Sally would have to decide, early on, whether she would offer personal help to those customers who could not find what they were looking for in the store. However, if she got into the habit of doing that, it would take her away from the Front of House role. So, instead, she determined to learn in what aisles each of the store's items were located so that she could direct customers where to find things rather than accompany them there.

A further decision made by Sally was that she would endeavour, personally, to resolve as many of the questions put to her by customers as she could, rather than, as a matter of course, merely refer them to other members of staff. In this way, she would be better able to engage with customers and establish a rapport with them. Also, she did not want fellow employees to feel that she was 'passing the buck'. Sally realised that she had to be careful since she had no experience of how Lidburys was managed; indeed, it was incredible to Sally that she had been given the job. The more she thought about it, the more unbelievable it seemed and the more she was determined to succeed. To do that she knew that she must avoid 'treading on the toes' of section heads and assistant managers or appearing to be a young upstart. She decided to face this, head on, by introducing herself to each section head and assistant manager and explaining to them that her role merely involved talking to customers and that she would let them know if she became aware of anything that might concern them. They were all receptive in one way or another although Sally thought some appeared to be wary.

Her objective, in all this, was to impress Mr Leigh and get a permanent position.

On Sally's first day of active service after her three-day garden chair vigil, she engaged with over fifty customers and had gathered details of a good number of these. With her Manchester accent and affable manner, it was not difficult for her to engage with customers many of whom had gone shopping only because they were lonely; not because they needed another carton of milk.

And this was another problem for Sally. Should she aim merely to be a greeter or should she also at the same time try to increase sales? The answer to this question was easy for Sally. If she was to generate the trust and confidence of customers then she should not allow them to wonder whether Sally might be there, principally, to get them to buy more. If she persuaded customers to make purchases (however small) that they really did not need or asked them for their address or email, it would be all too easy to risk losing their trust.

Customers' comments and questions, as expressed to Sally, did not vary much – *'the store is too cold'*; this or that item is *'more expensive than down the road'*; *'you do not stock begonias'* or *'why is the Returns Desk at the back of the store?'*

Something else she noticed was that while there were many customers who appeared to be lonely, strangely, there was little socialising between shoppers other, perhaps, than an occasional moan about the weather. Space was at a premium at Lidburys and they could not easily free up space for customers to enable them to meet. However, if that space were also to serve as a small profit-making café then a trade-off between, on the one hand, maximising shelf space and, on the other hand, increasing customer satisfaction by allowing customers to socialise could, she thought, be achieved.

Another plan of Sally's – which would not take up much floor space – was to erect a Customer Notice Board in order to help bring lonely souls together or advertise items for sale or promote a morning coffee club.

Sally sent an email to Mr Leigh every other day with her findings and recommendations and he responded promptly but with varying degrees of enthusiasm for her various ideas. In one email to Sally, he told her that her priority should be to keep up her dialogue with customers although he didn't know as yet to what extent this would have a positive impact on turnover or profit.

Sally was not put off and several of her suggestions (albeit the easier ones) were, indeed, implemented. A Customer Complaints Box and a Customer Notice Board were erected, as was a table to be used for the exchange of second-hand books which helped to improve Sally's relationship with customers if only because it would give her something else of relevance to talk to them about.

Looking back at the short period she had spent working in MacAmbroses, Sally realised that there had been no time, no moment, that she had not experienced a sense of unease there. As a new recruit in an unfamiliar environment it would have been natural to expect that time would be needed for her to learn how to navigate the uncharted tributaries of office life in a large City law firm. However, while she was there, she had always felt some kind of foreboding that she was imminently about to be summoned to account for some kind of mistake or even something worse.

On the other hand, after a few weeks at Lidburys, Sally felt completely relaxed. She had not experienced any need to look over her shoulder. The Manager was kind to her; he listened to her as if she had worked in Lidburys for years and she sensed that she was valued and respected. Her fellow employees put themselves out to help her whenever she asked and, furthermore, Lidburys customers were always polite and engaging. She was beginning to enjoy her Front of House role.

That was until something unexpected occurred; something which caused her to realise that she could not, by any means, take her position at Lidburys for granted.

On a Friday evening in January, two uniformed policemen came into the store. As Front of House, she was there to welcome them and to find out how she could help them – something she would be able to do without much effort because it was Sally, herself, to whom they wanted to talk.

*"Actually, **I am** Sally Bridge. How can I help you?"*

"Is there somewhere we can talk?"

The entry into the store of two uniformed police officers drew much attention and it soon got about that Front of House had been '*arrested*' and '*marched*' to the Manager's Office.

The officers behaved politely. They explained to both Sally and Mr Leigh that a Lidburys customer (they could not say who) had made a complaint that Sally had, that morning, stolen her purse. It was probably unintentional that the officers had divulged that the complainant was a 'she'.

The local police station would be investigating the matter and they would give both Sally and Mr Leigh further available information as soon as possible. With that they marched in a most policemanly-like manner out of the store.

Mr Leigh and Sally were left looking at each other. He did not say anything to Sally and it was she who broke the silence.

"I have no idea what that was all about … I can only think that, maybe, it has something to do with Ivy. She comes here every Friday morning even more confused than the Friday before … she must be in her late eighties. This morning she was particularly confused as to what, if anything, she wanted to buy and I had to take her to the bread counter. That's the only thing I can think of."

*"Sally, I know this is nothing, and I am quite sure the police will confirm that, but until then I am going to have to suspend you. It's Lidburys policy, and I just can't ignore it. I will ring you if I find out anything before **you** do."*

Sally was dismayed. How, she asked herself, could this be happening again?

Half the staff saw Sally leave the store two hours in advance of closing time looking ashen.

It was the following afternoon that the local police station called Sally at home to say that they had called the Manager of Lidburys to advise him that the complainant had now found her purse and that Sally could forget that anything had happened.

But Sally could not simply forget the shock and the humiliation she had suffered. Although she had been completely confident that all would be resolved satisfactorily she had been severely embarrassed by the incident.

That evening, Mr Leigh telephoned Sally, saying how pleased he was that the matter had been resolved so speedily and apologising again that he had been obliged to suspend her. He told her that Mrs Tarkani would set things straight about the incident among staff.

On the Monday, Mr Leigh was very welcoming to Sally. Strangely, he made no reference to the incident; he was clearly ignorant, she thought, as to the effect it had had on her.

He had called her into his office as he had something he wanted to give to Sally. It was a Customer Satisfaction Form he had picked up on Saturday extolling (in block capitals) her virtues:

"… OF YOUR FRONT OF HOUSE. SHE IS JUST PERFECT FOR YOU AND AN ASSET TO LIDBURYS. SHE HELPED ME SO MUCH ON MY LAST VISIT. DON'T LET HER GO!"

When she went to lunch Sally looked at the Customer Satisfaction Form and noticed that it was not the latest version used in the store. She knew about these things because it had been her job, only two weeks previously, to prepare the new form – boxes of the old version having been left in Mrs Tarkani's room for recycling.

After the Ivy incident, it took a few weeks before Sally could muster the courage to return to her practice of coming up with new suggestions to improve the store. Some of her past suggestions had initially been implemented but then dropped. They arose mainly from Sally's belief that supermarkets should be happy rather than humourless places for customers. It was usual for her to see the store's staff constantly scurrying round like mice while customers ambled along, often in a catatonic state, with their heads bent down searching for bargains.

She decided after a few weeks that the atmosphere in the store needed jollying up. Sally suggested introducing a series of in-store signs, which would generate (so she thought) some much-needed levity. She suggested, for instance, that the aisle which housed the toilet rolls and paper towels should be renamed '*The Aisle of White*' and that the toilets be renamed '**LOOM**' (short for '*LIDBURYS OF OLDHAM MEN*') and '**LOOS**' (standing for '*LIDBURYS OF OLDHAM SHES*'). 'The Aisle of White' idea was abandoned within three days and the idea of renaming the toilets did not even last that long since a lot of men had mistaken the '**LOOS**' for the gents.

Sally, over time, began to develop close working relationships with several members of staff and in particular with Mrs Tarkani, with whom she regularly went out for drinks after work.

After a further two months, Sally was offered a permanent position at Lidburys. Mr Leigh announced that he was very pleased with Sally's contribution.

"I think you are doing a great job here and we will increase your salary to £32,500 a year, backdated to when you started here. Is that OK?"

As Sally left his office, he called out to her to *"Keep up the good work!"*

And she did. It took another six months, but Lidburys found the space to set up a café which was used to host Lidbury events such as meetings of Lidburys Book Club and a Help Club. Lidburys was starting to establish itself as a small but effective civil hub which not only helped customer relations but also served as a small, but pronounced, uniting factor for the local community.

One evening in June, Mr Leigh and Sally found themselves leaving the store at the same time.

"Hi Sally. Have you time for a quick drink?"

They went to the pretty little Italian restaurant on the corner. They both had a glass of red wine and talked and talked, but not about work. Mr Leigh was eager to know a bit more about Sally and she decided there would be no harm in telling him her story. She felt comfortable in his company and she trusted him.

And so she talked to him of her recruitment by MI5, the ultimate act of treachery by Tony Forth (she did not mention his name), her traineeship – its beginning and its end – and that she had been disbarred from working as a lawyer. She also included the fact that she had worked at Lidburys as a teenager although under her sister's name. When she told him this, he laughed. She did not explain anything about her grandmother or her parents. That, Sally thought, would have been overmuch.

As Mr Leigh was paying the waiter, Sally wondered why she had mentioned **any** of her story to her boss, particularly since the whole sorry tale was self-deprecating and covered some very personal matters. However, she had felt the need to unburden herself and felt much better for it. There was also another element to this because by sharing a confidence in this way Sally thought that she might be able to generate a friend, and she was painfully aware that she did not have many of these – if, that is, we exclude the hundreds of Lidburys shoppers who would certainly count themselves amongst Sally's friends if they were asked.

And what did Mr Leigh think?

He had asked Sally to have a '*quick drink*' with him and had certainly not anticipated such an outpouring. However, he respected Sally for opening up to him about some obviously painful matters in a calm and composed manner and without any hint of self-pity. He did not think any the worse of Sally as a result. On the contrary, he was pleased to have recruited such an articulate member of staff to whom, he realised, he would be able, with complete confidence, to delegate all manner of responsible tasks.

He was also very flattered that Sally was prepared to take him into her confidence.

23.

SALLEIGH

As the days and months went by, Sally continued to shine in her role as Front of House.

She came to work early each morning full of enthusiasm and ideas for the performance she would be presenting to the shoppers of Oldham that day. Each day was slightly different – planned spontaneously by her as she travelled in on the bus.

Sally thought that regularly varying her presentation was the best way to enable her to maintain a freshness in the way she approached customers for they would soon get bored if Sally were to have the same conversation with them on each occasion they came into the store, whether that might be daily or weekly.

It was also important for Sally to maintain her own interest in the job and to inject a soupçon of nervousness into her role, something all good actors need to do in order to perform on stage to optimum effect.

In theatre-speak, Sally's title of 'Front of House' was thus misplaced because with each successive performance it was clear that a more appropriate label would have been *'Front of Stage'*.

There did not have to be much of a change in her performance for her to make a difference each day to her customers. Sally believed that little things made all the difference. For example, instead of always greeting one of her regulars with the question *'How are you today, Mr Piecroft?'* she would on some days accompany it with a statement such as *'Looking good this morning, Mr Piecroft'* or *'You are looking most sprightly this morning, Mr Piecroft'* and offer him an Everton Mint. Sometimes she would comment on the day's news, and sometimes she would ask after a customer's granddaughter or their arthritis or perhaps their cat. Sometimes she would stand the whole day facing **into** the store to speak to exiting shoppers and the next day her horizon would be those entering it. On occasions, she would discuss events which were going on in town or some momentous goings-on in *The Archer*s that week.

She knew that most regulars picked up on this and, indeed, they would often wonder on their way in what kind of greeting they might get from Sally that day. They told her as much.

In all this, Sally set two principles for herself.

First, she would try to avoid being condescending towards shoppers. That challenge would, for a lesser person, have been difficult to meet, but Sally cared; she had learned humility with her fall from grace in the law and had started to develop a real understanding of what life was really like for her customers.

Secondly, she would continue to ignore the recurring pressure on her in her role as '*Front of House'* to be a salesperson and was not prepared to recommend this or that product unless a shopper should specifically ask for her advice. She had regular discussions with assistant managers on this subject, since, naturally, they saw Sally as a valuable resource who could point shoppers in the direction of their particular department and their special offers of the day. Mr Leigh had once gently suggested to Sally that she might adopt this selling technique to see whether it would have an effect, however, Sally had effectively ended the discussion by telling him that, in her view, by asking the question – *'Why don't you have a look at the offers on the walking sticks in aisle 34, Mr Piecroft?'* she would more than likely *be* destroying months of effort to build up a trusted friendship.

Of course, Sally was aware that what she was doing as Front of House was no less a selling exercise than any other form of store promotion even though it might be less direct. This troubled her, and she sometimes had the feeling of being hypocritical. However, she squared this in her own mind by telling herself that she **was** part of the selling team (as every member of staff was) but that she perhaps cared that much more for her customers.

The fact that, month on month, there had been a steady increase in the store's turnover might have been the result of many factors and nothing at all to do with Sally, but Mr Leigh had a hunch that she was playing an important part. There was a different ambiance in the store. For reasons he could not identify, staff relationships and camaraderie were so much better; staff were much more eager to help each other out; and the atmosphere amongst customers was, he thought, quite different. Shoppers were more patient and polite to staff and he saw that they were more friendly to each other.

Mr Leigh was not the sort of Manager who would stint on giving his employees recognition where it was due. And so it was with Sally. One Friday morning after they had discussed one of Sally's reports, he asked her to have lunch with him at the little Italian on the corner. He wanted to congratulate her on her continuing dedication to the Front of House role and to find out how Sally was enjoying work. She was emailing him her regular reports but they did not include anything about her job satisfaction.

As they were looking at the menu, Simon – *"please call me Simon"* – asked Sally whether she was happy at Lidburys. They soon graduated, even before the arrival of their starters, to talking (as they had on their previous '*Italian*') about more personal matters, although on this occasion, Sally, having learned a lesson, just listened to Simon. He had not intended to talk as much as he did, but he realised that he felt very comfortable talking to her. Simon was not certain whether it had been at his or her instigation that their lunch break had ceased so quickly to be a purely business lunch.

As the couple sat together chatting merrily in the restaurant, it was, indeed, becoming apparent to Simon (helped perhaps by taking in more wine than he usually drank at lunchtime) that a change was developing in his attitude and feelings towards Sally. Whilst his purpose in inviting her to lunch had been merely to 'talk shop', he now felt more inclined to talk to Sally about himself. He had always been so disciplined in such things, maintaining a rule not to talk about himself to members of staff. However, he began to realise that this may well have been a screen for him to hide behind and to avoid revealing anything about his personal life; and he enjoyed being more candid. It surprised Simon that he might, at the age of forty, be learning something new about his own personality. It was, he supposed, Sally who had been the catalyst.

Blurring the line between work and personal life by engaging on a more personal level with one of his employees was one thing. Sleeping with a member of staff would be another. Nor was he certain whether Sally would be prepared to enter into a relationship with him, particularly since he knew her as a principled woman who maintained definite red lines. He knew how much she valued her job and that this was the most important part of her life, at least at present.

And so it was another three weeks before Simon decided what he was going to do. He asked Sally if she would go with him to a dinner party with some of his friends.

Sally knew that accepting such an invitation would be risky; she was in danger of complicating things at work by getting involved with Simon.

What is more, being in the company of complete strangers would make the occasion that much more daunting particularly since Simon had told her that all his friends were keen bridge players and Sally had no idea how to play card games of any kind. She knew that it would most certainly be uncomfortable for her, as a non-initiate, to be in the company of a group of aficionados engaged in animated discussion on an arcane subject to which she could not contribute a fig.

She knew, too, that she would have to be mindful of everything she said before she said it if she were to give herself any chance of impressing Simon and his friends and avoid making herself look foolish.

Sally was concerned that she was being invited into a 'lion's den' and this concern, combined with the awareness that she was not good at making new friends, was leading her towards refusing the invitation.

Simon recognised her reluctance and he promised her that he would look after her. She realised that it had been some time since she had been under the protection of **anyone**.

For his part, Simon liked the idea of having someone, having Sally, to look out for and protect; he had not felt this way for a considerable time.

By chance, the evening with his friends turned out far better than Sally expected.

Sitting opposite Sally, around the table of eight dinner guests, was Rhianne, her friend from school. They were so delighted to meet each other again after such a long time that the two of them grabbed the opportunity to chat whenever there was a quiet moment.

It was one of those occasions where, for the most part, each of the guests around the table listened attentively to whoever was talking at the time, thus avoiding the disagreeableness of everyone talking over each other and the disappointment of sitting at one end of the table listening to some tiresome conversation and missing a piece of gossip or a snippet of interesting information at the other end which appeared far more engaging. It was the most disciplined dinner discussion Sally had been invited to.

Prompted by the news that the Queen had, the previous week, become the UK's longest reigning monarch since her great-great-grandmother, Queen Victoria, a large part of the evening was taken up with a spirited discussion about the monarchy and how long it was likely to last.

"I, for one," said Simon, *"would like to see the size of the monarchy pruned. Unless we reduce the burgeoning number of those who have titles, the institution is bound to lose its public support and allure."*

"I agree," said another guest … *"the smaller the royal family the less chance there is of it tripping itself up."*

Rhianne disagreed. *"There will always be the potential for notoriety regardless of the size of the Royal Family. I think it has the unique ability to generate attention to the UK from around the world and the larger the family, the more opportunity it will have to increase that attention."*

Sally did not participate in any of that discussion. She was, instead, absorbed in reminding herself of the size of her **own** family. There was no other family she knew of with as few members as two. This brought her to wonder who her next of kin would be if Alice were no longer around.

Notwithstanding that one melancholic episode, Sally enjoyed the evening with Simon's friends. She had survived the evening intact; she had learned a lot about Simon, she had renewed her friendship with Rhianne and there had not, after all, been one mention of playing bridge.

To Sally's delight, it seemed she had sufficiently charmed Simon and his companions and she enjoyed gossiping on the phone with him about the evening the following day. They talked for over an hour and Simon thanked her for having accompanied him; he was gracious enough to tell her that it had meant a lot to him and that he had realised, only midway through the evening, just how tough an assignment he had put her through.

Sally had not realised that she had been on trial.

And they then started seeing each other regularly – at least three times a week.

24.
A BALANCING ACT

They would have to sort out how best they might balance their work and their private lives. Working together, on the one hand, and sleeping with each other, on the other, had to be carefully managed.

Sally, for her part, made a conscious effort to ensure that her friendship with Simon would not interfere with her job by making sure that no element of familiarity or casualness crept into her dealings with Simon at work or in her reports to him which could possibly indicate that they were in a relationship.

However, Sally's best efforts did not, ultimately, count for much, since it was difficult to keep secrets in an environment where everyone knew each other so well. While Sally was at all times scrupulous in saying nothing about Simon and her – even to Mrs Tarkani – it was that very uncommunicativeness, of which Sally could be very proud, that, in the end, let her down. Mrs Tarkani had worked with Simon for 14 years, and she could read him like a book. It was, therefore, not difficult for the astute Mrs Tarkani to recognise things which she had not previously seen. She noticed, for example, that while previously Simon would always greet Sally with a smile and a wave of the hand when she popped her head round Simon's door, such gestures, of late, were absent. It was also obvious to Mrs Tarkani that when the three of them were together Simon would go out of his way to avoid showing any familiarity to Sally.

Mrs Tarkani could also see that, correspondingly, Sally was appearing to ignore Simon. It was as if Sally was trying a bit too hard to make the point that not for one minute should anyone in Lidburys suspect that anything might be going on between the Manager and Front of House. It is not easy to lie effectively and neither Simon nor Sally had perfected the art – at least as far as Mrs Tarkani was concerned.

It was not too long before Sally's exemplary behaviour lapsed, at least in her own mind, in that she could not resist ending every report she sent to Simon with a kiss – that is, a camouflaged kiss – where the report would on each occasion end with a word which ended with an '*x*'. Last Monday, her report had ended with the words '… *and I will send you the Appendix*'. On Wednesday, it ended '… *but you might think that a bit unorthodox*' and she ended Friday's with the observation that some customers seemed unable to make a decision on what brand to buy because the choice was too great, something which she thought was '… *somewhat of a paradox*'.

Sally thought it most unlikely that anyone would spot this because they would not be comparing any day's report with the next. Sally was not even sure that Simon would notice; he certainly had not said anything to her that would suggest he had noticed any of her '*x-rated*' messages to him – but that did not matter, because Sally enjoyed such games for their own sake.

The only person who did positively know of the relationship was Alice who was keen to meet Simon, so Sally promised to find an opportunity for them to make each other's acquaintance as soon as possible. In the meantime, Alice did not stop nagging Sally.

But even Sally did not know that much about Simon.

Although they continued to meet frequently, with Sally often staying over at his flat in south Manchester, Simon did not volunteer much about himself or his family and Sally did not want to appear to be prying. They talked a lot about books and films and about Simon's friends and current news and politics. Indeed, they were more likely to discuss the first state visit to the UK of the Chinese President, Xi Jinping and the colossal programme which China had undertaken to build artificial islands in the South China Sea, than they were to engage in discussion about matters much nearer home.

Sally was beginning to think that this must be something to do with her.

Sally contented herself with the notion that they were 'taking it slowly', sensing a holding back on the part of Simon. Simon had gotten only so far as telling Sally that he was divorced. He had married young and had found, after three years, that he had little in common with his wife. It was, he said, a familiar story – they had gradually drifted apart having developed entirely different interests. Simon knew that having different interests could bring a couple closer, but not in this case.

*"My ex was a ballroom dancer, but I have no co-ordination or rhythm … no interest in dancing at all, in fact … I was completely absorbed with bridge, but she could not even **hold** a hand of cards. It is a pity … it wasn't my fault but it wasn't hers either. It sometimes happens like that."*

"What was her name?" Sally casually enquired.

"Why do you ask?" he gently chided.

"There's no reason other than I like to know people's names."

"That's something I've noticed about you," he chipped in, this time with a hint of criticism. *"You always start a conversation with a stranger by asking them their name, even when the odds are that you will never meet them again."*

"I suppose that's an occupational necessity if you work as Front of House; but I have always been like that. I've got this thing that I can't begin to talk to anyone unless I know their name. And with my nearest and dearest, it is a way of showing affection. To hear one's name being used is like being hugged or touched. It

enables us to make and strengthen connections with each other whatever our relationship might be."

"Without using our names," she continued, *"we cannot effectively relate to each other; without having names for things, we can't talk about them properly or give them an existence. Things are nothing if they have no name or label because without that you cannot identify them. It's a matter of identity. That's why Adam gave the animals names right at the beginning of things. It **is** the first thing. But it's not merely a biblical thing. It's also about being pragmatic. If a label falls off an item in your store, it will lose all value. Even if a customer knows what the item is, she will put it aside because she doesn't know what its price is or whether it's vegan or gluten free or made in Peru. It can get discarded all for the want of a label."*

"Wow!" replied Simon, again chiding her, *"I didn't expect such a long response. You have made me think – and I will check in future that all our labels have an extra degree of stickiness!"*

Sally did not rise to the bait, although she was irritated by Simon's dismissiveness – as well as the fact that he had still not revealed his ex-wife's name.

And that was the way it often went with them. Sally would start off with a question or an opinion about something she thought was worth discussing; Simon would deflect it; Sally would not be able to resist mounting one of her hobby horses, and Simon would sign off with some sardonic comment which, only by accident, would end with an $'x'$.

So Sally did not know where she stood with Simon. If he were to ask her to marry him any time soon, she thought she would accept and that they would probably 'live happily ever after'. He was handsome with delicate features, blue eyes, sensitive hands and a well-proportioned body, although he was just a little shorter than her. He had the most beguiling smile and a deep velvety voice, but he had the habit, at times, of being too introspective. He was also, on occasions, impatient and often interrupted people – not **her** so much, but that, she thought, could also happen in time. As she had just witnessed, he was often dismissive of what she believed were her more serious moments.

She knew from what Simon had said that he had gone through a long string of women friends since his divorce and she had no idea whether she might merely be just another section of that string rather than the end of it. She used that metaphor when speaking to Alice, joking with her that she thought Simon was probably 'just stringing her along!'

But it was **not** a joke.

If Sally was merely a temporary diversion for Simon then she needed to know since she did not feel comfortable with indefinitely postponing the start of a family any more than postponing a decision on her career path. Whilst she was most happy with her current job, were she to break up with Simon, she knew that she would not be able to continue to work at Lidburys with him.

This uncertainty was unsettling and was exacerbated by Sally's suspicion – and it was no more than a suspicion – that Simon was seeing other women.

It was not that she had noticed any unfamiliar perfume or foreign lipstick on his shirt, but something far less conclusive. Call it a hunch. It was merely that the previous week while they were driving to Simon's flat he had idly asked Sally what seemed to her to be an odd question. He had simply asked her whether she had managed to find her dry cleaning ticket. She politely informed him that she had not used a dry cleaner for months, and he mumbled that he must have been thinking of his mother.

Several things then happened which should have reduced Sally's feelings of insecurity.

Alice had found two flats in south Manchester in a newly-built block. The flats met the requirement as to the proximity that Sally had insisted on – in fact, they were next door to each other on the seventh floor.

They were both so relieved to be able, at last, to leave their one-bedroom hotel accommodation and to move into their own separate two-bedroom apartments. As much as she had enjoyed living in the hotel with Alice, she realised how much she had missed privacy. It was not only a matter of privacy but also of freedom and independence. Living together in one hotel room meant that they were both forever behaving in accordance with how they imagined they should behave rather than the way they each wanted to.

The move was particularly convenient for Alice, who had found a job as a trainee in a nearby travel agency and was taking to it 'like a duck to water'. With Sally's encouragement, Alice had, it seemed, found her perfect calling.

All this was going on at the same time as Simon was, unexpectedly, given promotion to a larger

Lidburys in Heaton Park, Manchester which he would be taking up in three months' time.

◆ ◆ ◆

One late Tuesday afternoon, on Simon's day off, someone had died in the Oldham Lidburys. It was one of the sub-managers, Mr Gregorio, who had suffered a fatal heart attack on aisle 16 – garden furniture. Sally was first made aware that something was wrong when a customer complained to her that she could not get access to buy a deckchair. She accompanied the customer to aisle 16 and sure enough found a 'roadblock' halfway down the aisle consisting of three large red erected umbrellas placed to prevent further access. Access was similarly denied from the other end of aisle 16 and in between there appeared to be a lot of subdued activity. The staff in that section were adamant that Mr Gregorio should not be moved.

Sally did not have time to examine Lidburys protocol for dealing with occurrences such as this, but she instinctively knew that she could not allow a dead body to remain on a supermarket floor with shoppers milling about. She could not speak to Simon or locate any assistant manager so she took it upon herself to do what she thought correct, namely, to close the store until the sub-manager's body had been taken out of the store. That involved a public announcement and the co-operation of the staff.

As the store emptied, Sally got word to the staff that this was not as serious a situation as a bomb having been left in the store, so that there was no need for any panic just an orderly exodus.

She could not even tell anyone whether Lidburys would be opening again that evening, which is what those customers queuing at the checkouts most wanted to know, and so she decided that they would be allowed to take their items home with them and come back the following day to pay for them. That one particular demonstration of trust had helped to clear the store of most customers very quickly.

Taking matters into her own hands in this way had been risky. Sally was only Front of House and some members of staff thought her actions were ill-conceived. Some resented her for taking control. Sally, indeed, was worried what Head Office might say.

In the upshot, ninety-five per cent of those customers came back into the store over the following week to pay for the items they had taken the previous Tuesday. Whether they under-reported their purchases was another matter.

Sally learned a lot from that episode. She was particularly struck by the customers, who, in the following weeks, had gone out of their way to tell her how impressed they were with the way she had handled matters.

Simon was, of course, upset about Mr Gregorio, who had been a valuable member of the team, but he was delighted to learn how Sally had dealt with things so effectively in his absence.

She would have preferred to hear that from Head Office and, indeed, she soon did.

Head Office got to know everything that had happened that afternoon from the report that Sally had prepared for Simon (ending with the words '… *which I have just put into your letterbox'*) and had sent a long email to Sally telling her that they were impressed with how she had reacted in a difficult situation and that they were in the process of updating the Store Manual accordingly.

A month later, she was asked by Head Office whether she would be prepared, now Simon Leigh had left to go to his new position at Heaton Park, to become an assistant manager of the store. For someone who had been at Lidburys for no more than a year (if you ignore her earlier year and a half stint as a shelf-filler), this rise in the hierarchy was completely unprecedented and it was that much sweeter for it.

Although she certainly missed Simon's daily proximity, Sally thought that, in many ways, it would be easier for the two of them if they were no longer working in the same store. At least this is what she hoped.

However, it seemed to Sally that now Simon was working in the Heaton Park store their relationship had shown signs of cooling – at least on Simon's side. She was already seeing Simon less regularly.

Sally thought that there was certainly an indication of such a cooling when it came to the possibility of Alice and Simon meeting each other. Despite Sally's gentle initial nudges and then the application of some more pronounced pressure by Sally, Simon continued to resist. Sally could not understand Simon's prevarication. Conceivably, this was Simon making an oblique point to Sally with regards to his commitment to her; maybe he was prioritising his precious time; possibly he was merely indulging his selfishness – he certainly

271

knew how important this was to Sally; or perhaps this was the stance of a man who was excessively concerned with maintaining privacy in his life. Alternatively, maybe this was just Simon indicating that it was he who was in control.

Although Sally suspected that it was because she and Simon were no longer working in such close physical proximity that their affair was cooling, she did not know for sure. She knew only that **her** feelings for Simon had strengthened since he had taken up his new position.

Sally thought that there might be several explanations for the apparent change in their relationship other than that it might be coming to an end. Simon's new position in Heaton Park involved much more responsibility than did his managership of the Oldham Lidburys and Sally knew there was a large amount of new information he had been obliged to absorb, not only about the wider range of products but also about the running of a much larger workforce, consisting of several tiers of management, which were not supported in the Oldham store. Obviously, Simon needed to show that he was up to his new job, and this must have made it more difficult for him to devote the same amount of attention to her as he had done previously.

But she knew that she was constructing flimsy excuses on behalf of Simon and she fretted and became depressed, particularly because she had half expected Simon to ask her to join him as Front of House in Heaton Park – but he had not raised that possibility with her.

Simon's track record for maintaining relationships with women was not a good one and Sally continued to be troubled by her suspicion that Simon was not interested in any long-term relationship with her. If that were true then Sally would end things with Simon immediately and so she began to rehearse what she would say to him when next they met.

She had planned 'to dip her toe in the water' before advancing to a point where she might say something she would regret. She was concerned that talking to Simon about the robustness of their relationship might be the very opportunity for Simon to 'bust' it.

Simon called Sally late one evening to ask her if she would have supper with him the following day; he would pick her up from her flat and take her to a newly-opened trattoria in Heaton Park. He was as friendly as he always was on the telephone but, such was Sally's state of unrest, that this looked to her as if it was indeed to be the occasion Simon intended to end things. That fear was compounded by the fact that he had told her that he could speak only for a few minutes and did not account for why he had not made contact with Sally for three days.

Sally had not previously heard of the restaurant, which was called '*La Bella Donna*' – was this a portent? Was this to be a nicely rounded-off affair starting and ending with an Italian restaurant, she asked herself?

Sally had decided that, to maintain her self-respect, she would need to get in first, and once they had ordered their meal, she told Simon that she had something to ask him.

"Before you ask me," Simon interrupted, *"I have something to ask **you**, which is even more important!"*

It may have been that that momentary display of assertiveness on Simon's part had, at the very least, saved Sally much embarrassment and had perhaps avoided the immediate ending of their relationship, since what Simon wanted to ask her was whether she would be prepared to go over to meet his mother for supper on Thursday next week.

As soon as she had taken in the significance of that question, the tension in Sally's body began to ease, beginning with a relaxation in her neck and shoulders, a process assisted by her taking a large gulp of red wine.

Sally knew that for most men a gesture of this kind would mean that they had some idea in mind of a long-term relationship. In Simon's case, though, it might merely be the result of an overbearing mother who was overly concerned about her 40-year-old son and inquisitive about the current woman in his life.

Simon had spoken of his mother and it was clear that he listened to her; it was also clear that she was a fine cook. So, heedless of the precise workings of the machinery that had driven this unexpected invitation, she promptly accepted. Sally could not remember the last time she had eaten a good home-cooked meal which had not been made by her. If she had coped with '*a lion's den*', she could surely cope with that of a lioness.

"I'm so pleased. Next Thursday it is then. And what was it you wanted to ask me, Sally?"

"Oh, I wanted to ask you how your new job was going."

"Well, I can't say that it's a walk in the park; it's more strenuous than Oldham and I really miss not having you around."

Four days later, Simon came to the Oldham store to pick up Sally so that she did not have to go back home to her flat to change. She had brought in a change of clothes that morning and showered in the store.

"Are you at all nervous introducing me to your mother?"

"Not really. I am sure she'll like you. You get on with everyone."

"Have you told her much about me?"

"She doesn't even know your name," he replied without thinking.

Unless he was joking, this was the cruellest cut to Sally, since it implied that his relationship with her was not after all that important to him and that he had not been influenced one jot by her diatribe a few months ago about the importance she put on using names.

She stepped into Simon's mother's apartment in south Manchester feeling somewhat miffed about this, however, her miffiness, or whatever she might have called it, was soon dissipated.

Simon hugged his mother and stood back to introduce … but before he could begin to do so Rosemary exclaimed loudly:

"Sally! Sally! Sally! I don't believe it! My, what a wonderful surprise! Come in and take your coat off immediately."

Simon felt a little neglected and in the excitement was nearly left outside the front door.

"I suppose you know each other then?" he asked sardonically. Now it was **his** turn to be miffed.

Neither of his women had heard his short question, since they were far too pre-occupied with hugging each other and, in the case of Rosemary, crying tears of surprise and delight. It appeared as if this were a scene in which mother and daughter, separated from each other for many years, had unexpectedly been reunited. Who could have guessed that they had last met only a few months ago on a train and had no family connection.

Of course, Simon was completely bemused by this outpouring of joy. In truth, he was somewhat relieved that he did not have to make yet another introduction and that, for once, his mother looked pleased with his dinner guest.

They sat down and drank a lot of wine. Simon looked alternatively at his girlfriend and his mother, expecting some form of explanation from them – either of them – since the wind had been taken from his sails. He had been carefully practising what he was going to say to his mother by way of introducing Sally and he had anticipated all of the reactions which might have been his mother's – except for the one that had just occurred.

Sally glanced at him and felt a bit sorry for him.

"We owe you an explanation, Simon; you see your mother and I met on a train journey in May 2012, when she saved my life. That's not me exaggerating or being over-dramatic; that is truly the position – you will remember that I talked to you about that awful day."

"I'm rarely speechless," replied Simon, *"but it can't often be that a mother knows more about her son's woman-friend than **he** does. Did neither of you know you were going to meet each other this evening?"*

Rosemary interrupted, *"Of course not, silly, do you think I would have been able to keep this from you? I am one of Sally's biggest fans and had I known you were seeing each other, I would have asked the two of you over long ago."*

Although Simon took a while to thaw out, the three of them were soon in high spirits and having much more fun than any of them had anticipated.

Rosemary had expected to suffer a long and awkward evening while trying to keep the conversation going; Simon had expected his mother would, as usual, be friendly though distant and that he would be frequently embarrassed by her; and Sally – well she had not known **what** to expect, except that she had not expected this.

An evening that was billed as an 'ice-breaker' turned out to be more of a 'matchmaker' because, without Rosemary being too presumptuous, the entirety of her conversation with her son and his girlfriend was grounded on the assumption that their relationship was long term.

25.
CI

Two momentous events followed in quick succession.

Sally and Alice each received large cheques from Mr Chambers in respect of their parents' estate. Apart from briefly discussing this event with each other, they told no one of the money.

Mr Chambers enclosed with the cheques his detailed calculations explaining how the payments had been worked out, but Sally could not bring herself to go through them. Mr Chambers might, Sally thought, have made multiple errors in those calculations, but she decided (without sharing that decision with Alice) that she would leave the verification to her sister – and Alice did likewise.

Whether this lapse was based on complete trust in Mr Chambers or laziness on their part would have been difficult to determine, particularly since that determination would have been made even more difficult by yet another factor, namely, their embarrassment at being in receipt of such a large amount of cash as a result of a tragedy rather than from the efforts of their own labour. They had not contemplated wealth of such a dimension, and to be in receipt of it was a shock to them both.

What was an even greater problem for them was the decision as to what they should do with the cash because their embarrassment gave rise to a reluctance to consult a financial adviser or even to look to Mr Chambers for help.

The second event (placed second by Sally merely by virtue of chronology and not because of its relative significance) was the decision by the UK to extricate itself from the European Union.

A few days after that momentous event, Sally received an envelope in the post addressed to *'Ms Sally Bridges'*. Enclosed was a cutting from *The Daily Telegraph* newspaper dealing with the consequences of the UK vote in favour of leaving the EU. Along the top margin of the cutting, which had been neatly scissored to size, were written in red the words *'Sally, I thought this might be of interest to you'*.

The writer was wrong. While Sally was passionately interested in politics and deeply concerned about the outcome of the Referendum, after hearing months of Brexit noise, she had no interest in the article.

And yet she became completely obsessed with it.

Sally soon developed the certitude that the cutting had a significance far beyond the arena of politics and any shift in world power.

Sally was well aware from her studies that there will be many reasons why we might need to scrutinise any particular piece of text – each investigation having its own distinct purpose. We might be interested in reading the text in order to develop an understanding of what the writer has to say; or to learn the text by heart; or to analyse its meter; or to translate it into a foreign language; or to examine the font used in the text; or to proofread it for spelling or grammatical errors; or, if we were its author, to revise the text so that it more clearly represented our intentions; and so on and so on.

In reading and re-reading the newspaper cutting she had none of these purposes in mind; instead, she was merely searching for the clue which she was convinced was hidden somewhere in the article. But what might such a clue be intended to lead to? She had no idea what she should be looking for.

She had regularly lost herself in the process of unravelling crossword clues, but this was an entirely different exercise. Before she could even contemplate solving '*the clue*' she would have to identify whether any such clue even existed and then of what it actually consisted. Sally's long entanglement in cruciverbalism had taught her when to give up on an impossible clue, but that experience provided no succour here. She frequently had the urge to turn to page 42 to find the answer – but there was no page 42 here and no answer.

She knew full well that she should stop '*beating herself up*', but the compulsion continued to take a tighter hold. The more often she resolved to take fire to the cutting, the shorter was the interval before the next occasion she sat down to examine it in yet another forlorn effort to solve the so-called puzzle.

After almost two weeks of on and off effort, Sally decided that enough was enough and she summoned her dwindling resources to summarise what she knew (or thought she knew) about the cutting in one last-ditch effort to resolve matters.

She did not even have any idea who had sent the cutting. Maybe it was merely the gesture of a well-meaning friend. But she had few friends, none of whom read *The Daily Telegraph*. In any event, a friend would surely have added their name. This convinced her that the cutting was not from a friend so she could not simply ignore it.

It was more likely that it had something to do with Tony; perhaps the cutting had been sent by a former colleague of Tony who was tipping Sally off about his whereabouts. But in that event, what could be the purpose of supplying her with any information – and why such secretiveness? Was the message written in red to indicate urgency? If Tony had cheated a partner in crime and taken off with their ill-gotten gains, how could she be expected to help?

Perhaps the cutting had been sent to her by Tony himself. That was unlikely because the envelope in which the cutting was sent was addressed to *'Ms Sally Bridges'* as opposed to

'*Bridge*' and Tony would have known the correct spelling of her name. In any event, how would he have found her new address? And what possible relevant information about him could be contained in an article about Brexit?

Sally was beginning to despair and threw the cutting on the floor. It was a matter of chance that it fell '*Brexit down*', since what then caught Sally's attention, for the first time, was an advertisement for cosmetic surgery on the reverse of the cutting. What she found in that advert did not much advance her search, but it did strengthen her resolve not to give up – at least not just yet – for the advertisement referred three times to a '*clinic*' and in the last of them, there appeared to be a mark under the first letter 'c' and the second letter 'i'. The markings were faint, but under a magnifying glass there was no doubt that someone had intended to underline those two letters. Sally felt vindicated, even though her week of anxiety had merely revealed two faint pencil marks.

Was this an indication that Tony might have undergone surgery to disguise himself, or should she concentrate on the 'C' and the 'I' or was it the other way round – 'I' and then 'C'?

That the cutting might have something to do with cosmetic surgery seemed to Sally most probable. She returned to consider her theory that any clue would refer to a town or a place. If that was correct, then the possibility that the '*clue*' was 'IC' appeared remote, as all she could find with those initials was 'The Ivory Coast', which was, indeed, too remote. It was more likely that the clue – if a clue it was – was constituted by the initials 'CI', in that order, if only because that led to many more possibilities; in fact, five of them. A quick search came up with several island groups: 'The Christmas Islands', 'Coney Island', 'The Canary Islands', 'The Cayman Islands' and 'The Channel Islands'. Sally was excited, even invigorated – this was better than finding the solution to an elusive crossword clue. She had taken a massive step in her journey, although she was no further forward.

She poured herself a glass of *Glenmorangie* single malt Scotch to relieve her tension.

She would reach some conclusions on the matter based on what she knew and then, once and for all, cease her endless ruminations. She decided that:

- The cutting had been sent to her by a person with a grudge against Tony Forth.

- the purpose of this was to encourage her to locate him or flush him out.
- That person had been cheated by Tony Forth.
- The envelope had been sent by someone in the UK.
- The 'CI' was a red herring; and
- She would keep her eye out for anything which might suggest she was under observation by anybody.

These all appeared to Sally to be reasonable conclusions. For now, she told herself, she should rest and she poured herself another generous glass of single malt.

26.

SALLY AND TONY

Sally had not received any communication from Simon since their Thursday evening supper at his mother's a few days earlier.

Despite all the other things going on in Sally's life, she had found time to work out exactly what she was going to say to Simon should his silence, as she anticipated, signal a termination of their friendship.

Sally was becoming increasingly angry that, even if there was a reason for him to be upset with her, Simon had not had the civility to call her. This was, to Sally, so petulant of Simon that the longer the stand-off continued, the less inclined she felt to call him. Why should she do so when she had not done anything which could be criticised?

In the process of fathoming what was happening with Simon, something else occurred to Sally which she thought was telling. She suspected that she might perhaps be nearly as angry with Simon for jeopardising Sally's friendship with Rosemary as she was with him for his behaviour towards **her**.

At the same time as Sally was thinking about all this, she realised Tony Forth had managed, unknowingly, to hijack any inclination she might have to mend her relationship with Simon.

A few days after Sally had managed to cobble together her final conclusions regarding *The Daily Telegraph* cutting, she received the following letter in the post from Tony Forth:

Dear Sally

I know that as soon as you open this letter and see that it is from me you will want to destroy it. If you haven't yet done so, please hear me out. It must also be a shock to be hearing from me after such a long time, which I tried to soften by sending you that cutting from the Telegraph.

I can't hope to excuse my atrocious conduct in leaving you without notice, without saying goodbye and not contacting you for such a long time. There is no possible way that I could repair any of the hurt that I must have caused you. I have no excuses. I was motivated by greed and I let that base characteristic get a hold of me to the point where I am now thoroughly ashamed of myself as a human being - I could excuse you for thinking that I haven't yet even reached that level.

I am much wiser now and I understand how far I have fallen below what you had the right to expect from me irrespective of the temptations which life throws in one's path.

I have been incarcerated here in Grand Cayman in prison for money-laundering offences, and I might be entitled to early release subject to what I say below. I am desparate [sic] to get to Glasgow to see my father, who has only six months to live. I am telling you this not as a sob story but to earnestly seek your assistance because my early release is conditional on being able to *prove that I was previously in MI5, something neither the British Government nor anyone else is able (or perhaps prepared) to say anything about. You are the only person who could now possibly assist me. All that would be necessary from you is a short statement.*

I will understand if you are not prepared to help me, but I am pleading with all my might for you to help me out here.

I know that you must have scores of unanswered questions. I will answer anything and do anything. I am desparately [sic] in need of your help.

Pleadingly,

Tony Forth

Sally's reaction on receipt of that astonishing letter so long after they had last spoken was multifaceted.

She was, firstly, dismayed that it had forced her to confront issues which she had long ago put to rest. She then experienced hatred for Tony Forth, to a point that neither the distance between them nor his imprisonment would have prevented her from doing him physical harm had it not been for her next response – abject pity. This was followed by a desire for revenge. On the smorgasbord of emotions served up to Sally was also her anger that Tony Forth's letter was so casual and so familiar as if they had last been in touch only the previous month.

The letter had an overwhelming effect on her and for days she could do very little, so wrapped up in herself had she become – wrapped up, that is, by a mere A6 sheet of thin prison notepaper, the contents of which had assaulted her so painfully.

But she had not been completely immobilised by the letter, because she was able to find the space to make plans for a long trip abroad and to do some letter-writing of her own:

Dear Tony

You can have no possible conception of the havoc you have brought to my life and I do not propose wasting any time amplifying that.

You have an unbelievable amount of gall in writing to me and even more in making demands of me when it is me who should be making demands of you.

Nothing could compensate for the damage you have done to me, but do not even contemplate deriving any satisfaction from that because I have now overcome the adversity which followed your crass, objectionable conduct - the behaviour of a self-obsessed juvenile coward.

That you are selfish beyond all belief is demonstrated by your own hand - every paragraph of your pleading letter beginning with the same letter of the alphabet.

But I will not be dragged down to your level. Explain to me what you want me to write, and I will write it.

However, I have some conditions:

1 When you reach Scotland, you will, for at least one year, take a job in a supermarket of my choosing, stacking shelves.

2 That you will never make any effort, yourself or through any intermediary, to make contact with me.

3 *Whether or not they want you to, you will report once a week to a police station.*

4 *You will write me a detailed explanation of what was going on in the build up to your departure from London. I need to have a full understanding of your deception.*

5 *For that year you will deposit all your passports with me.*

Mrs Sally Hardcastle

Writing that letter had a profound cathartic effect on Sally, enabling her to recover her equanimity and to enjoy a period of tranquillity during which she was able, if only temporarily, to put an end to some of her demons.

She did not need to receive any reply from Tony Forth, since she had learned from **his** letter all that she needed to know in order to be able to live in her own skin and under her own name.

In any event, she would never have received a reply, since although she had penned it and corrected it and proofread it and folded it neatly into a carefully addressed envelope, she had never intended to send that letter to Tony Forth – nor did she.

Instead, she sent something else to him. What she posted to Tony Forth was a scrappy piece of crumpled newsprint torn unevenly from a newspaper, bearing Tony's own words, *'I'm sorry'*, on the back of which could be found part of an advertisement for Filofax diary refills. If you were to look most carefully at this you would have been able to see a faint pencil mark under each of the first and fourth letters of that word – and the clear deletion of its final letter.

27.

SIMON LEIGH

If there is anything which is destined to fester in the mind of a grown man it will be the thought that he is being controlled by his mother. In the hierarchy of infestations, this, Simon thought, was even more disturbing than being manipulated by a girlfriend.

What Simon could not put out of his mind was the suspicion that his mother had been well aware of his relationship with Sally prior to their meal together the previous Thursday. This had led him to the inevitable conclusion that Sally knew that she was going to meet his mother that evening. Simon concluded that both mother and girlfriend had been duplicitous in saying nothing about their friendship in advance. The fact that Simon had enjoyed the evening would make no difference to the conclusion he had come to – he could not abide being controlled by anyone. Nor could he cope with being left standing alone outside in the hallway. He thought that, in effect, this had rendered him merely a witness to his own existence.

Even worse, he thought, there is nothing more destined to dampen a man's affection for his girlfriend than the notion that she had lied to him. He might forgive his mother that, but not his girlfriend.

And so, that cosy Thursday supper, which on the surface would have led any discerning wall-fly to suppose that it would be the making of a fine couple, was, in practice, the breaking of a fine couple, since Simon, wrapped up in the misconceived belief that he had been dealt some awful wrong, had made no effort to contact Sally for a period which had now extended to seven days.

We can ascribe haughtiness, perhaps pride, on the part of Simon as the likely cause of that breakdown, but to do so would be to ignore something of far greater significance, something far more harmful than hubris and which has the ability

SIMON LEIGH

to blight any relationship, whether a personal friendship, at one end of the spectrum, or an international peace treaty at the other.

Thorough forensic analysis would likely produce a wide range of possible conclusions as to the culprits or the causes of the breakdown of any relationship so that seeking to identify any one reason would unlikely be profitable. Yet there is one particularly malign influence that regularly presents itself and that is the occurrence of some kind of misunderstanding.

Simon's misreading of the true circumstances which had occurred at his mother's home that evening was just such an example.

It would not be the only misunderstanding to disrupt Sally's life, but this one could possibly be of Shakespearean proportions – not that Shakespeare has a monopoly, since so abundant are misunderstandings in everyday life that we might wonder why the curriculum at home, school or university does not devote a little space to help us identify and minimise at least some of their more egregious consequences. Seeing that we all have a natural predisposition to react without thinking, to jump to conclusions, to nurture preconceived ideas and to wallow in our own prejudices, such a line of education might not take us very far in this endeavour. Until a Masters course in Misapprehension is set up somewhere, we will not know for sure.

For her part, Sally, after seven days of radio silence, suspected what might be its cause since she was aware of how acutely Simon had reacted when it became clear to him that his mother and his girlfriend already knew each other.

But what could Sally now do to repair things? To speak to Rosemary about her son would make things worse. Yet, to call Simon would be to suggest that Simon had done nothing wrong.

In such a zugzwang, all that Sally could think of doing … was to do nothing; or perhaps she would wait a few more days and then telephone Simon.

Simon Leigh was a mercurial fellow. Not even his mother, who loved him unconditionally, was quite sure how he worked. If you wound him up, his reactions would be hard to predict – even for his mother – and so it was no wonder that Sally was so surprised at the manner in which Simon had reacted at that inauspicious Thursday night supper.

Had Sally and Rosemary discussed the outcome of that evening with each other, they would have reached the same conclusion, namely, that Simon's reaction was a lot to do with his pique having peaked. How else could one account for Simon's anger towards his mother, on the one hand, and his boorish neglect of Sally on the other?

We might posit that, faced with the same circumstances as Simon Leigh had been presented on that Thursday evening, most men would, following initial surprise, have immediately let out a hearty laugh, for it is of such serendipitous occasions that relationships can be forged. But Simon, even at the youthful age of forty, was set in a mould of his own making and could not bring himself to apply humour to a situation which, to him, was not funny.

Had Simon enjoyed the gift of a cinematographic memory, he would have been able, on playback, to see that all the evidence on that evening pointed conclusively to the fact that his mother had told him the truth when she said that she had no idea that it would be Sally who he would be bringing for supper that evening.

Simon was by no means certain how he felt about Sally and he had perhaps been unconsciously hoping that his mother would (as she had done in the past with most of the other special supper guests he had brought over for inspection) be less than fulsome in her comments about Sally. If Rosemary had indicated any coldness towards Sally, then that that would have been the justification for Simon terminating his affair with her. Indeed, coldness or disinterest was what he was expecting his mother to show towards Sally and he was discomfited when the complete opposite occurred. It was as if his mother was making the decision for him.

When it came to his dalliances with women, Simon found it difficult to make his own decisions; and yet he also found it hard to accept the advice of others. This was the nub of it. Whilst his indecisiveness regarding his choice of women was so ingrained that it could be resolved only by means of subcontracting decisions to someone else (usually, his mother), he would act on that subcontracted decision only if he agreed with it.

Simon barely knew his own mind regarding any of his affairs with his many women. He tried but found it difficult to be honest with himself let alone with those (such as his mother) with whom he was so close.

Simon was not a natural 'chit-chatterer' and would have benefited from some kind of academic course (here we go again) in the art of idle banter – a discipline which everyone would benefit from in order to make progress in their relationships, whether at work or at home. This was another of the attributes he had noticed in Sally – not only was she adept at chatting to the diverse group of Lidburys customers, but she had also been brave enough (as she showed when they had enjoyed their first drink together) to volunteer the most intimate details about herself. Simon would never be able to do that.

And so it might be thought that Simon would find that Sally and he, while not necessarily compatible, **did** complement each other neatly, since those qualities dead or dying in him could be found blossoming in her.

Adding to the large pile of 'plusses', Simon knew Sally to be intelligent and loyal, gregarious and very attractive. If he were to be looking for a mate, what more could he expect?

However, having learnt a lesson in the case of his first wife (his mother was most encouraged whenever Simon referred to her in this way) he knew that it was vital for him to be able to share some genuine interests with any woman he might now commit to. But he found that there was little indication that Sally and he could achieve such communion. There was the possibility that the two of them would be able to share plenty of intellectual pursuits such as music, reading and films, but Simon was afraid that Sally was far too intelligent for him; and he thought she talked too much about matters which she considered important but which he did not. They did not have sufficient 'common heritage' or 'commonality' – he could not quite put his finger on it.

Maybe it was much simpler than that. When Simon asked himself the question whether he should continue seeing Sally, he had to battle with the possibility that *'he did not think he was in love with her'*. He told himself that *'he **should** have been'*, but he was not – or at least *'not yet'*, these being two words he had recently added to his vocabulary in thinking about all this.

At the same time as he was going backwards and forwards, forwards and backwards, contemplating his true feelings for Sally and when it might be appropriate for him to call her, Simon received a phone call from an unknown caller which did more to make up his mind about Sally than any call he might have received from the most trusted confidant.

"Hello, is that Simon Leigh?"

"Yes, who is that?"

"I need to contact Sally Bridge urgently, can you please give me her telephone number?"

"Who are you?"

"I am afraid I can't tell you that, but I can assure you that it's extremely urgent."

"And I am afraid that I can't give out personal details without knowing who ..."

But before he had finished his sentence, the caller had put down his phone. Simon could not locate the caller's number.

Simon was disturbed by this bizarre call. How could any caller have believed that it would bear fruit? What should he do? He decided immediately and with no help from any sub-contractor that he would text Sally to warn her.

"Sally, I apologise for not being in touch earlier. Pl. excuse me and I will explain. In meantime you should be aware that I rcvd a strange phone call just now asking for your tel. no. which I didn't of course give out. The caller refused to say who he was. Simon x."

Sally texted back immediately. *"Did his voice have any distinguishing characteristics?"*

"It was a short conversation, but I think he might have been an Aussie."

Whether out of guilt or as a result of a surge of affection brought on by the menace of the phone call, Simon immediately wrote a long and ardent letter to Sally apologising to her for his rudeness and seeking to explain it. It took him well into the night to prepare it and it was compelling.

It would be interesting to know how Sally would have reacted to it had she ever had the opportunity to read it.

28.
BREAK-IN

Sally suffered from BES – that is, '*Brown Envelope Syndrome*' – which describes the propensity to put such envelopes aside without opening them and then to ignore them. She had, over the previous six months, received six manilla envelopes from HMRC. Whether out of fear, laziness or stupidity (it was, in fact, all three), Sally would, on receiving them, immediately place each unopened envelope behind her pair of Shelley Blue Dragon vases on the small oval table which stood in the hallway to her flat. It was the perfect place to stash them – hidden from view when she came home but nonetheless sufficiently open to view each time she left her flat to ensure that she did not **completely** forget them.

She knew the provenance of the six letters – that was obvious without having to open their envelopes – but since she had always had tax deducted through Pay As You Earn and had not previously filled out a tax return, she had persuaded herself that the letters could not be of any importance. She had too many distractions in her life, too many other things to worry about, to find time now to open them.

And then she was visited by yet another unwelcome distraction – a burglary.

She had returned from work early one Friday afternoon to find the front door of her flat slightly ajar. At first she thought that Alice must be visiting her flat, but Alice was in Italy. Opening the door wider but with some trepidation, she could see that the flat had been ransacked. Anxious and dismayed that her new flat had been vandalised, she went about trying to identify what had been stolen. The police came round that evening, spending half an hour with her asking a series of questions to which she was unable to supply any meaningful answers. In particular, she was unable to tell the police officer whether anything had been stolen.

"It seems to me, Miss, that they were looking for something. There is no sign of a forced entry, so that

points to a professional job by someone who has picked your lock. Has anyone else got a key?"

"Only my sister next door, but she's abroad at present ... oh god, I've not checked her flat ... what if they got into hers too?"

As Sally was going off to investigate, she noticed that the six unopened manilla envelopes hiding behind the Shelley Blue Dragon vases were no longer there. She could not have known that the carefully crafted letter from Simon, which had arrived that morning on her doormat after she had left for work, was also missing.

"Wait a sec, there **is** something missing. There were several envelopes on the table this morning but they now seem to be missing."

"Were they of any value?"

"I doubt it."

"What do you mean?"

"Well, they were only unopened letters from the taxman."

The officer scribbled in his notebook as they all went next door. Nothing appeared to have been touched in Alice's flat.

The officer gave Sally a crime number and left.

Sally was shaken. She immediately called a locksmith and arranged for him to call the following day to change the lock and fit an additional one.

She spent the rest of the evening clearing up and looking to see what else might have been stolen. She could not find anything missing, although she hoped she would because the idea that she had been targeted, or that there was something specific which the thieves wanted, frightened her a great deal. What she found peculiar was the fact that the six letters from HM Revenue & Customs had disappeared. The two Shelley vases must, she thought, have been worth more than those letters.

The more she thought about the burglary, the more she became concerned. She could not help thinking that there must be some connection with the call that Simon had received the previous day. Before going to bed that night, she wedged a kitchen chair securely against the front door.

She decided that the break-in must be something to do with Tony or one of his confederates, but how and why now? It was so sad, she thought, that she could not even bring herself to seek the comfort of Simon in her ruminations and it was unfortunate that Alice was once more away when Sally needed her.

And then she had a thought. Could the thieves have been looking for her black notebook? She knew it contained details of conversations she had had with JJ. That was it, she thought; that is what this is all about. Thoughts were now occurring to her as if she were being pelted with an unending series of snowballs. She rushed into her bedroom, which is where she thought she had hidden her notebook when she had moved into the flat six months previously. But she could not find it. The cutlery tray! she thought and ran into the kitchen to see if it was still there.

It was – and yet it wasn't.

There **was** a black notebook under the motley array of kitchen utensils, but when she opened it, she did not recognise it as being **her** notebook.

She settled down in the kitchen with a glass of wine to examine it. Her recollection was that she had used up only a fraction of hers, whereas this one was almost completely full – full, that is, of hieroglyphics, which would clearly take her time to decipher – if ever she could.

She then recalled that when she had left the Mildmay flat that night in 2012, she had initially believed that Tony must have taken her notebook only, in her frenzy, to come across it (or what she thought was her notebook). Of course, she told herself, Tony had not meant to take **her** notebook but had grabbed it, in haste, thinking it was **his**. She, for her part, had taken his notebook thinking it was **hers**.

Her mind was in turmoil. Was it **her** notebook they were after? Or was it Tony's?

She slowly turned the pages of Tony's notebook even though she could not understand more than a few words in it. She suspected that it contained many treasures, but no simple 'open sesame' would reveal what was in **this** Aladdin's cave.

First thing the following morning she booked a taxi to a safe deposit in Addington Street, where she put Tony's notebook into a secure deposit box which she opened for the purpose. She hurried back to be at home for the locksmith and when he had finished his work, she congratulated herself that she had accomplished a lot that day.

Considering the task that lay ahead of her, Sally had, in reality, accomplished next to nothing.

The following day, as of a whim, she prepared a letter to Lidburys of Oldham, explaining that, for personal reasons, she had decided to give in her notice and that she was so very sorry to be leaving them in the lurch.

But this was not entirely a whim, for she had in fact been thinking what she should do for some time. She had not enjoyed working there for some months; she had been finding it difficult to concentrate and she had become bored with supermarket life. She much regretted not giving them proper notice, but she justified her shortcomings by telling herself that Lidburys was better off without her declining level of performance.

29.

REFLECTION IN RUTLAND WATER

As soon as Alice had returned home from Italy, Sally went next door to tell her of the break-in and Alice, too, called the locksmith.

The news of Sally packing in her job at Lidburys seemed to surprise Alice even more than the news of the break-in, despite Sally's explanation of how very disenchanted she was with her job.

It did not take long for Alice to realise how churned up Sally was and that she needed some immediate therapeutic attention to bring her out of her doldrum. Without telling Sally in advance, she booked a weekend for the two of them in a country house hotel in Rutland. Alice planned to hire a small car to get them there and they would return home on the Monday morning.

Sally was delighted with Alice's plan and saw on the hotel's website that it was an elegant, isolated mansion with its own lake and gardens.

"This should easily lift the spirits, Sally!"

Indeed, it turned out to be just the kind of hotel they were hoping for – a place where they wouldn't be bothered by anyone.

Alice planned a few long walks for them. Saturday's expedition was a 10-mile hike through field paths, farm tracks and country lanes, which took them along Fort Henry Lakes, through Tunneley Wood and Westland Wood into the village of Exton. The air was warm and sweet and the birdsong pronounced. For the first two hours, they ambled rather than rambled and talked of nothing but inconsequentials.

*"Did you know, Sally, that though Rutland is England's **smallest** county, it has the UK's **largest** man-made lake, which we can visit tomorrow. Although the Kielder Dam in Northumberland disputes this. Actually, they are both right because Rutland's lake is bigger in area and Kielder's is larger in volume – so there. I looked that up last night to impress you, Sally!"*

"Forever the little tour guide, aren't you, Alice!"

Alice could not find a suitable segue and decided to dive straight in.

"Sally, do you feel like talking?"

There was a pause while they navigated a metal kissing gate and then Alice continued.

"Do you think you will repair things with Simon – you seem to have so much in common with him."

Sally halted and stared at Alice.

"Why do you ask me that? Has someone said something to you – have you been talking to Rosemary?"

"Of course not. I was wondering whether Simon might still be the reason for your depressed state."

"Well, you're right. I am thoroughly depressed. But I don't think that's merely Simon's doing. I really don't think he's the right person for me, all the more now I see how petty he has been and how self-absorbed he is. Although he appears, on the face of it, to be straightforward and transparent, he's a difficult person to fathom … Simon is totally self-centred and I don't believe that he would be able to find proper room in his life for me as well as him. He is like the word 'me', which is a simple everyday word we all understand, but you try and produce an effective dictionary definition!"

They came to a succession of stiles and turnstiles and, both in deep thought, they walked in silence for a while. Out of nowhere came Sally's observation.

"I think that Simon may be Jewish."

Alice stopped abruptly. *"So?"* – It was a short riposte, but by means of both the rising intonation and a sharp intake of breath, it was instrumental in conveying, at one and the same time, a negative response, an indication of disinterest and also a question – all three at the cost of only one syllable.

Alice continued. *"There – you **are** still thinking of Simon; why do you think he might be Jewish?"*

"Well, during that train journey from Euston which I am always wittering on about, Rosemary talked about lighting candles on a Friday night and it occurred to me, only recently, what that probably indicated."

"That's a bit of a conclusion. Maybe she just likes lighting candles."

*"What, only on Fridays? Besides which, I once saw an envelope on Simon's desk which was addressed to Simon Dovid Leigh'; that **must** make him Jewish!"*

"Would that make any difference to you?"

"Not at all! I was just thinking."

"… of Simon?"

"No. I've been thinking about our grandparents."

"Do you mean their being Jewish? Because that's also been on my mind. Until the Coroner's hearing, I had been totally unaware of anything about our grandparents and certainly not that they had both suffered in concentration camps in Poland. I feel so terribly sad and so awfully guilty that I never talked to them about any of it."

"Don't be stupid! We were not even 10 when grandma died. Even if we did have the maturity to understand things at that age, which I much doubt, do you think that grandma would have engaged with us? Ma's secrecy was born of grandma's. She would never have told us a thing," replied Sally forcefully.

"OK, but you'd think that she might have given us **some** *idea of the Jewish connection."*

"There was, and still is, much more than a 'connection'. I think you will find that if Ma's parents were Jewish then that would have made Ma Jewish and that if **she** *was Jewish then, technically, so must we be."*

They sat watching barn swallows preparing for the first part of their 6,000-mile flight to South Africa – if only the victims of persecution had enjoyed such a prospect.

"But how can we be Jewish," Alice enquired, *"if we have not had a Jewish upbringing of any kind? In fact, I doubt whether the word 'Jewish' was ever mentioned in our house when we were kids. If it was so important, why did Ma do her level best to keep it hidden from us until after she had died? It's as if Ma was so ashamed of her religion that she could not even admit her own existence. It's much too late now. I've no interest in any of it."*

*"I can't understand it either ... and that's what's eating me up because I really **would** like to understand."*

They walked in deep contemplation for a field and a half.

Her eyes looking down at her walking boots, Alice broke the silence.

*"And what do you think Ma meant when she referred to the 'Imber dynasty'? Did she expect that we should go off and create busloads of kids or was she referring to Jewish kids? Is that what she was hoping? Ma was so far off the scale that it's impossible to put meaning into anything she did or said. I couldn't go as far as to say that it is 'eating **me** up' in any way; it all feels so remote that I feel untouched by the idea that there might be some nascent corpuscles of blood circulating*

around my body that might be awakened to make me someone different from the person I feel myself to be."

Alice was less inquisitive than Sally. Or perhaps it was not a matter of lacking inquisitiveness but more that she was just a different soul who did not have the same need as Sally to reach an understanding of herself to be able to live a fulfilled life.

Sally took the Ordnance Survey map from Alice, who had, up till now, been the group tour guide, and stepped in front of her to take over.

Alice was sensitive enough of her sister's moods to know that there were occasions when she should give Sally plenty of space, and so they hardly spoke for the rest of the day – even during their evening meal. Alice knew that Sally was so deep in thought that to disturb her would be as rude as it would be to awaken her from a sweet, dream-laden sleep.

No doubt as a result of their walk, Sally was, indeed, now in a kind of self-induced trance. She had been absorbed for several months in trying to work out what it was that was troubling her or, at least, what was troubling her the most.

At the end of each day, Sally always itemised in her head (if not also in her diary) her priorities for the next day. She was also inclined to ponder on her longer-term goals and the obstacles she thought she had to face. If she was lucky, she might, on some nights, be able to wipe the slate clean. However, over the past few years, she had found it more difficult to do so. That was because she was beset by an intrusive ever-present fog of varying density which had enveloped her to the point where she thought she might be going into depression. It was a fog of a kind which made it difficult for her to identify what was unsettling her and that, in turn, made her doubt the effectiveness of her powers of introspection – powers of which she had previously been quietly proud. She was still uncertain how she should deal with Simon; she also needed to work out what kind of job she should be looking for, now that she had left Lidburys.

The day's physical exercise helped Sally fall sleep quite easily that night. However, that ease was not matched by either the length or quality of her night's slumber, for she awoke suddenly after only two hours' sleep. She could not recall having any particular dream, but she was aware that her sleep had not been trouble-free. As she sat up in bed, in the darkness, she eventually came to the realisation that it had been something that Alice had said the previous day which was playing on her mind.

Alice had said something about nascent corpuscles of blood circulating around her body (or rather **not** circulating around her body). Perhaps it was not red or white, or any other shade of blood corpuscles, but certainly it was something equally as real, such as an electric current running loose in her brain which had the ability, without her knowing, to work on her subconscious and affect both her hours awake and her hours asleep.

Sally certainly had an urge to know who she was and she thought that this was probably what had been troubling her rather than the trauma of being defrocked, or the shock of being duped, or the humiliation of (it seemed) being twice-dumped. Each of those debasements had a beginning and, she hoped, an end, and each had a cause which Sally could identify – that is, if she chose to.

Having no clear identity was not a debasement of the same kind as her other debacles – it was much worse. It was certainly worse than **losing** your identity because at least in that case you would know what you had lost. But if you have never **had** any kind of identity, then you would quite possibly conclude that there wasn't one to be had or at least not one that fitted you, or ever could fit you.

These thoughts had been troubling her ever since the day of the Coroner's hearing, but she had sublimated them, perhaps because it was too painful a subject to be let loose amongst her conscious thoughts. She had not even had the sense to talk it over with Alice and she knew that this weekend must be the right occasion.

Before she could talk to Alice, however, Sally needed to consult with her own self – even if it was four in the morning. She had lots of questions to think about, all emanating from the revelation that she came from Jewish grandparents. She needed, in particular, to confront the fact that her grandparents obviously knew of their identity as Jews throughout their lives but were totally committed to hiding it, whereas, in complete contrast, **she** had not had any idea of her heritage until recently but might now decide to invigorate it.

What had it been like for her grandparents growing up – particularly her grandfather living in Poland? Sally wondered if she would be able to find whether, somewhere, there was a family tree, or should she create one? Why did her grandparents forsake their religion? Was the reason for that the same reason her mother had hidden **hers**? Is that why she had killed herself? Would it be possible for Sally to learn what it meant to be Jewish? Could Sally properly bring up any children of her own without being able to answer questions of this kind?

Sally thought that investigating issues such as these might well be akin to her setting off on yet another excursion, one which would involve the negotiation only of blind alleys because that is what her life had consisted of, so far. She knew, only too well, what it was like to invest time and effort and love (or any combination of them) in an endeavour which would eventually turn out to be a fruitless meander down a cul-de-sac; but, nonetheless, she felt compelled to undertake that journey.

As a child growing up in Ashton-under-Lyne, Sally had not been challenged by her family, her school or even herself to address the question: *'Who are you?'*

She had received plenty of encouragement to think about questions such as: *'What do you want to be?'* and *'What do you want to achieve?'* but they were very different questions. Perhaps, thought Sally, it

325

was just as well that she had not been challenged in this way, because she would have experienced as much difficulty then as she had now in answering the question: '*Who are you?*'

Sally's parents had never prepared her to consider such a question because they themselves would not have been able to answer it – either for themselves or for their daughters.

At breakfast, Sally and Alice agreed that their walk that morning would consist of a scenic tour of Rutland Water, circumnavigating the Hambleton peninsula and ending up in *The Finch's Arms* for a drink.

They talked initially about Alice's travel business. Despite its problems and cash shortages, it had grown in a short time into a secure, thriving enterprise with offices in Manchester and Leeds. The Manchester office, with retail premises situated below, specialised in holiday travel to Turkey and the Leeds office dealt with business travel. Sally was aware that Alice was now fluent in Turkish, and she asked Alice lots of questions about her recent trips to Turkey and also about her forthcoming business trip to Izmir.

But Alice was most anxious to continue their conversation from the previous day – as indeed was Sally – and Alice brought a quick halt to the travelogue.

*"Changing the subject, you didn't say yesterday what **you** thought Ma meant by the 'Imber Dynasty'."*

"I really don't know," replied Sally, *"although I have been thinking a lot about everything else you were saying yesterday."*

"And …?"

*"I agree with your description of Ma. I don't think I ever understood her, either, and that is precisely why I've now got this urge to understand **myself** better, and in order to do so, I feel I must find out more about where our grandparents were from, who they were and what they did. When I have children I want to be able to explain to them where their family originated from and who they were. And I don't intend to keep anything from them. Can you understand that?"*

Alice was thinking how to reply, but Sally did not give her time.

"In the meantime, I am playing snakes and ladders with my life. I don't seem to have a man in my life; I don't have any profession or business. I have no passion and no purpose; I don't belong to any clubs or even to a choir or anything; nor do I have any religion; and, apart from you, I don't have any close friends."

Sally's diatribe progressively increased both in intensity and volume as she enumerated each additional shortcoming.

"Bloody hell, Alice, I haven't even learned how to drive! ... Frankly, I have no idea where I am or even **who** *I am. I lived for years as the second born and then suddenly find out that I have become the elder of us. One moment I am floating above it all in splendid isolation and the next moment I am down, sinking in self-disgust."*

Alice did not know how she could effectively counter any of that and they just sat there together in silence on a bench overlooking the lake, fascinated by the Egyptian Geese, who were enjoying the water one minute, the trees the next and, all the while, making out that they were really ducks.

"What do you think you might do now you've decided to leave Lidburys?"

"I don't know – but I've come to the decision that I'm going to put aside the next six months to find out what it means to be Jewish and to investigate the Imber family history. I have already started. I found out this morning that the name 'Imber' is a Yiddish name derived from 'ingber' (with an 'ng' instead of an 'm') which means 'ginger, in Polish – so I'm already making good

*progress! You said yesterday that you had no interest in all this and that your Imber blood doesn't inspire you. I can understand that, but I must tell you that **mine** does; and I know that if I don't explore it now I will always regret it."*

Sally continued.

"I think I might embark on an entirely new career – I don't know what, but I have several ideas, including setting up in business as a mediator, which I think would suit me quite well because in recent months one of my tasks as assistant manager was to resolve disputes between the supermarket and senior members of staff. It has been the one thing I have really enjoyed and I think that I've been moderately good at it. Shuttling backwards and forwards between the parties and trying to get into their minds without imposing my own has been invigorating … or perhaps I will become a genealogist or perhaps … I just don't know at the moment ..."

… and with that she proceeded to sally forth down the lane, out of Alice's earshot, striding purposefully towards *The Finch's Arms*.

30.
DODGING BULLETS

What Sally could not have realised was that the break-in was one of the luckiest of all the adversities to have befallen her. Had it not been for that, she would once again have used the two Shelley Blue Dragon vases as a mask for the seventh manilla envelope which arrived on her doormat a few days after the trip to Rutland.

It had been Alice's fate as a kid to suffer the loss of her sense of smell. Sally suffered from a variant of that ailment in that, from time to time, she would lack the sensitivity to sniff out when things were not quite what they should be. It was a serious and, indeed, costly affliction. This sensitivity had failed her when she was taken in by Tony and again when she had failed to sense that something was afoot in Manilla – but luckily the break-in had cured the disorder.

She opened that seventh letter from HM Revenue & Customs immediately and sat down to read it.

Dear Miss Bridge,

As you are aware from our previous letters, HMRC have information that gives us reason to suspect that you have committed tax fraud …

Sally read the word '*fraud*' and nothing more was required to render her almost catatonic – she had to pause for breath before she could take in the rest of the letter. Her failure to open any of the six previous letters made it difficult for her to understand the seventh, so she had to read the letter half a dozen times before she could make **any** sense of it.

It took several minutes before she could compose herself and look at the booklet that was enclosed with the letter – *Code of Practice 9 HM Revenue & Customs investigations*. Sally was trembling too much to take it all in but it appeared that HMRC had decided to investigate her for fraud using (COP9) (a frightening acronym in itself, she thought). In short, she was to be given the opportunity to make a complete and accurate disclosure of all irregularities in her tax affairs and if HMRC were satisfied she had done so, then there would be no criminal prosecution.

If she did not believe that she had brought about a loss of tax, she could sign a Rejection Letter, in which case HMRC would initiate an investigation that could be a criminal investigation. She also read that there was a possibility of penalties up to 200 per cent of the tax due.

She was slowly able to arrive at some provisional conclusions.

First, Sally knew that she had done nothing wrong.

Next, she could not neglect the latest letter from HMRC as she had done their earlier letters. She realised how stupid, how very stupid, she had been and that it was no wonder that HMRC had taken such a tough stance – she had ignored their communications.

Thirdly, she would not take any specialist advice. The whole thing was obviously a big mistake and she could handle it with a telephone call or two. Her concern was only that the booklet said that HMRC were unable to enter into any discussion about a taxpayer's tax affairs until they had notified HMRC of how they wished to proceed. Despite that, she would try and so she called the number on the letter, hoping to speak to a D J Channing. She got through first time and gave the reference on the letter.

"Hello, my name is Sally Bridge and I am phoning to apologise and explain myself. Can you spare me ten minutes?"

Miss Channing was equally polite and said she would call Sally back as soon as she had acquainted herself with the details. Sally was delighted to have made such quick progress and took the time to do what she should have done previously – make some notes.

Miss Channing called back half an hour later and although Sally was expecting the call, she jumped when the telephone rang.

"As I mentioned, I am phoning to apologise to you for not responding to your earlier letters. I received your latest letter yesterday but, for reasons I will explain, I have not read any of your earlier letters and so have no idea what I am accused of. The truth is that I was

negligent in not opening your earlier letters, but I no longer have them – they have been stolen."

Sally wondered if what she had just said sounded ridiculous.

"Miss Bridge, until you decide whether you are or are not going to proceed via Code of Practice 9, you will appreciate that I cannot have a conversation with you. I called you back simply to find out why there had been such a delay in your responding. What I would strongly recommend is that you instruct an adviser to guide you through what is a complex issue with serious implications."

"Thank you for that," Sally replied, *"I know of absolutely nothing which I might have done that could remotely be said to involve fraud on HMRC and I don't want to spend precious money on an accountant. I am quite certain that if you are acting on information received, that information must be mistaken."*

"As I say, I suggest you get advice and decide whether you will proceed via COP8 or COP9. Once you decide on that we can take the next step, but until then I am afraid there is nothing more I can add."

And that is where matters came to rest. Sally had not even managed to use up one half of the ten minutes she had requested.

Sally immediately wrote to Miss Channing, once again apologising for the inexcusable delay and explaining that the earlier letters to her had been stolen. She included the crime number for the break-in and her signed Rejection Letter, saying that she hoped that it would now be possible to hear back from Miss Channing as to what it was that she was being accused of.

Within a few days, she received a response from Miss Channing to the effect that HMRC would be pursuing a criminal investigation against her concerning substantial funds in an undisclosed overseas bank account in Sally's name.

Oddly, Sally was encouraged by this reply because it was an indication (so she thought) that this was simply a case of mistaken identity and that there must be another Miss Sally Bridge out there who should be experiencing this traumatic journey in place of her. She replied to Miss Channing accordingly. Much to Sally's surprise, the immediate response was that it was, indeed, **she** who was the proper subject of the enquiry and would she please attend a meeting accompanied by her adviser in London on the 14th of next month at 3pm. This letter made no sense to Sally, who was scared, confused and feeling so utterly vulnerable. How could this be happening to her?

Sally was already feeling a formidable weight on her and she knew that she would not come out of this nightmare well unless she had someone to give her support – that support would ordinarily come from Alice to whom Sally would naturally turn in such a crisis, but Alice was in Izmir and would not be returning to Manchester until the night before the proposed meeting with HMRC. Sally was eager to avoid having to change the date proposed for the meeting and in the hope that Alice would be able to go to London with her on the 14th to 'hold her hand', she would immediately email her.

In the absence of Alice, there was only one other person to whom Sally could turn.

31.

BEN ASHCROFTE

The only fellow trainee at MacAmbroses with whom Sally had kept in contact was Ben Ashcrofte whose judgement she highly respected. He had worked in the tax department and Sally could not understand why he had left to engage in an entirely different branch of legal work. They had chatted several times on the phone over the past few years, but she had not told Ben any of the details of her departure from MacAmbroses.

She decided that she would explain her current predicament with the tax authorities in the hope that he might be able to give her some guidance. She would text him first to find a convenient time for her to call and would tell him the whole story.

He knew a lot of it already – particularly about what had happened in May 2012 and the subsequent enquiry by MacAmbroses. Everyone in the firm knew; it had been impossible to keep it quiet. Ben was eager to talk to Sally about her departure from the firm, not to engage in gossip but to reflect together on their shared experiences, to re-invigorate their friendship. He was aware that what Sally needed most was to talk to someone who would understand.

"Would it help," he asked, *"if we started with the aftermath of the United Pedals saga?"*

Ben thought he knew the basic thinking of the firm.

MacAmbroses had been severely shaken by the revelation that they had invited a *'mole'* into their midst. That in itself was a serious embarrassment. Even greater was their public discomfiture as a result of the leak of confidential information on the takeover of United Pedals and the consequential investigation by the Financial Conduct Authority. The firm had gone into 'damage limitation' mode and had set up a team to report on what had happened and how best to avoid a similar debacle recurring.

They decided that since they could not prevent the facts from coming into the public domain they would make a virtue of necessity and share everything openly with the whole firm. Ben told Sally that he thought this was an unusual (and perhaps risky) approach but one which he thought had helped to reduce the fall-out.

Part of the report was taken up with the question as to whether it would be wise to demand of trainees (and indeed of everyone working in the firm in whatever capacity) that they declare any membership or association they might have with any branch of the security services. But the report went on to consider why they should stop there. Why not go on to ask them whether they might be a member of any group supporting independence for Scotland; or an anti-vaccination activist; or a spy for some foreign power?

It did not take long for the firm to decide that it would not be profitable or practical to delve in this fashion into the proclivities of those who either wanted to join MacAmbroses or were already working there, not merely because there would be no end to the questions which could be asked of them, but also because there would be no way in which the firm could rely on the veracity of the answers they might receive. A McCarthy-style witch-hunt could never be effective; besides which the pool from which MacAmbrose were recruiting was possibly the least likely to contain subversives, blackguards, knaves and varlets so that the risk of enduring a similar experience was not high.

Rather, their answer was to be as thorough as they could in their vetting procedures; to use trained interviewers who could 'smell trouble' at a hundred paces; to invest more heavily in training and by being frank and open, hope they would be able, in return, to rely upon the integrity and trustworthiness of their personnel.

That was all very well, however, if (as seemed clear) one of their trainees had been an MI5 agent, MacAmbroses could not ignore the possibility that there might be others. They owed it to their clients (as well as the whole firm) to do as much as they could reasonably do to determine whether there might be other 'moles' in the firm and to get rid of them.

All efforts to accomplish this task through the security services were likely to (and did) come to naught, and the firm had to engage in more direct action. They decided that the best place to start would be on the cohort of trainees recruited by the firm in 2011. Everyone in the firm was aware of the *cause célèbre,* but the uncertainty which it had caused had fallen more on the 2011 trainees than on anyone else simply because Sally had been one of them. The firm certainly wished to avoid creating a toxic culture, however, it decided that they had no alternative but to announce that *'it would be making all necessary enquiries'*. The purpose of this was not to initiate a witch-hunt but simply to encourage any remaining miscreants to leave of their own accord. Indeed, one trainee did terminate her traineeship early, but she had a plausible reason for doing so – a serious heart condition – so that those in the firm looking for an endgame were not satisfied by this outcome.

"We constantly felt that we were under surveillance – and we probably were!"

Sally felt very uncomfortable being reminded so vividly about a time in her life she had been trying so hard to forget and she was keen to move on.

"Ben, what I really need from you is whether you have ever come across Tony Forth."

"Who's he?"

"He was the person who recruited me."

*"I don't know him, but I think I should tell you something that I have wanted to tell you for a long time … it is that I, **too**, was recruited by MI5…"*

Sally had not been expecting that revelation.

343

"… I was recruited by someone called Alan Field. It's hard, isn't it, to believe that the security services would have more than one agent doing this kind of work!"

"You may have to suspend belief even more," Sally responded quickly, *"because Alan Field and Tony Forth are one and the same. You and I were recruited by the same person!"*

Sally and Ben exchanged details about the Field and the Forth to enable them to verify that they were, indeed, the same person and Ben continued.

"Well, I suppose we shouldn't be surprised. He is difficult to fathom. I had hardly any contact with the man at first but then he started to call me to chat and we occasionally went out drinking together, just the two of us … this was while you were still at MacAmbroses… and we struck up a kind of friendship; well at least that's what I thought it was. But it soon became clear that he was using me."

"My immediate problem," Sally interjected, *"is that HMRC have decided to prosecute me because of an undisclosed foreign bank account and ..."*

"… are you referring to an account that Alan Field … Tony Forth … (whoever he is) set up for you?"

That question left Sally speechless. How did Ben know? It seemed everyone knew about the bank account before she did – Tony Forth knew, HMRC and now Ben Ashcrofte.

"How is it that you know anything about this? What more can you tell me? Why do you think that Tony Forth set it up? I can't believe this!"

"Well, I was telling you … It was soon after you'd left MacAmbroses that Field made contact again asking for random bits of advice. On one occasion he told me that he needed to set up a foreign bank account for someone and wanted to know where and how he could do this without revealing his own name. Well, I can tell you, he got into a right mess. He couldn't decide where to set up the account or which bank to use and when he did finally decide, the bank he had applied to simply refused to work with him. It was at that point that he emailed me for urgent help attaching – obviously by mistake – a long string of emails, including one which referred to 'Miss Sally Bridge'. I couldn't be sure, but it was pretty obvious that the bank account he had been talking about all along was intended for you. However, by that time I'd become completely disenchanted both by MacAmbroses and Alan Field. Daily life at MacAmbroses had become unbearable for us trainees – although I must say that I was more concerned that Field might try to manipulate me in the same way as he

obviously had got to you, and so, in short, I decided it was time to get out from both. I've had no contact with Field since leaving, and I never found out whether the bank account was actually set up."

"Well, unfortunately, it was," Sally replied bitterly. "So it wasn't **you** who spilled the beans to HMRC about the bank account?"

"My god, no! Why would I have done that?" and he paused.

Sally took in a deep breath.

"Do you think it was Tony Forth who informed HMRC?"

"Why should he have done that when it must have been him who opened the bank account in the first place? Although I despise the man, I don't think it's likely to have been him ... although I can tell you I would never trust him; and after the stunt he performed in recruiting me, nor would I ever talk to him again."

"Was he ever part of MI5?"

"I thought you'd ask me that because that was something I had been asking myself. I have been dying to speak to you about all this but didn't want to broach the subject. When he originally recruited the two of us, I am pretty sure Field must have been working for the security service but, from what he once volunteered to *me, I suspected that he must have been kicked out although there is no way we are ever likely to find out!"*

"And what about Tony Forth's team of accomplices?"

"Who are you referring to?"

Sally described the dealings she had had with JJ and Alex Carstairs and her suspicions. The telephone conversation with Ben was making her feel even more confident that she could continue to trust him and she felt that the more details she divulged, the more likely it was that he would be able to help her.

"I don't think I've heard of either of them; Field never mentioned either of them to me, at least by name, but from what you are telling me about what happened to you, it certainly looks like they were in league with Field and that perhaps he double-crossed them. If that's right then it's quite plausible that they are still looking for their share of the proceeds and that it was JJ and Alex Carstairs who contacted HMRC. They needn't have had any accurate information to pass to them. They could possibly have been acting on a mere hunch that you were involved in some way and that, if so, you would probably have stashed your proceeds somewhere overseas. It's called 'stirring it up' to see whether they could pick up anything of interest. It's an old trick and even if any

such hunch was totally misconceived, they would have nothing to lose from trying it on."

It was as if Ben had then suddenly run out of steam.

"Well, it's been good to talk again, Sally, but I have to go. Please call if you need anything more from me. I am around all next week."

Sally would have liked to talk to Ben for much longer; there were still so many unanswered questions. She was bursting to know more about Ben's experience as one of Tony Forth's other recruits; she had failed to ask Ben anything about the new firm he had set up; she had not got round to telling Ben that Tony Forth had written to her from prison; they had not spent any time exchanging information about their personal lives; and she had not asked Ben whether he had ever met the blonde with the streak of pink hair. Ben had been too keen to wrap things up.

What Ben had told Sally made it most likely, in her eyes, that it was either JJ or Carstairs, or both of them, who was responsible for the break-in. What made all this worse was that, if that was correct, they now knew of the HMRC investigation and would be delighted that their hunch (if that's what it had been) had paid off. It would encourage them to pursue Sally.

She berated herself, yet again, for her stupidity in ignoring those manilla envelopes.

Sally spent a lot of her time thinking about the forthcoming interview with HMRC and how she should deal with Miss Channing and this inevitably brought Sally back to thinking about Tony.

If, contrary to what Ben Ashcrofte had said, it **was** Tony who had been the informant then perhaps, thought Sally, Tony had given the money to her as a '*Trojan Horse*' so that he might use it at some time as a stick to beat her with or to get some kind of hold over her. Sally thought that Tony might, indeed, have been the one who had informed HMRC of the existence of the bank account; she thought he might have done so out of spite because she had failed to respond to his request for help. It was difficult to work out who else could have known about the account – unless Tony had told someone else about it. That was certainly possible she thought; after all, he had told Ben Ashcrofte.

32.

TO LONDON AND BACK

Following her telephone conversation with Ben Ashcrofte, Sally had to confront how she would deal with the possibility – maybe now the likelihood – that JJ or Carstairs would again interfere in her life.

She hoped that if JJ and Carstairs still wanted information from her they would be satisfied merely with **talking** to her, however, the break-in indicated that they might be prepared to resort to violence of some sort, and so Sally resolved to take some further precautions by carrying in her bag both a pepper spray deterrent and a loud, pulsating alarm device.

That was just as well, for one evening as Sally was leaving the supermarket, she was accosted by JJ. He appeared to Sally to be unkempt – either in disregard of his former smart grooming or perhaps helpless to achieve it – which made him all the more intimidating to her. He approached her, took hold of her elbow and asked her if she would accompany him to the coffee shop across the road 'to clear the air'. Notwithstanding her anticipation of trouble, Sally was stunned by his appearing in this way, and unthinkingly she allowed herself to be led to the coffee shop just a couple of minutes away.

Sally used that time to think of some kind of strategy. She decided that it would not be wise to make a scene or make a dash for it but that she would give the best impression she could of being totally calm and unconcerned.

They sat opposite each other at a large round table chosen by Sally, in the middle of the coffee shop, and she opened her bag and placed it on her lap. She thought it unlikely that JJ would try anything in a public place but would take no chances.

"What would you like to drink?" JJ asked when a waiter approached.

"Nothing," she replied gruffly.

Sally thought that she would attract more attention from the staff if she were to refuse to drink anything.

"I won't beat about the bush. I have reason to believe that you know the whereabouts of the cash that Tony Forth has stolen from me and if you don't tell me where it is, there will be some unhappy consequences."

Sally did not respond and JJ continued.

"I believe you and Tony have conspired to keep my share of the money and I will not rest until I get it. Do I make myself clear?"

"What you say is quite clear and I will try to make myself equally as clear in the few minutes which I have before I will be getting up and walking out of here. Firstly, I have no idea where any money of yours might be. Secondly, I am not part of any conspiracy with anyone – let alone Tony Forth. Thirdly, if you come anywhere near me or my flat again or make any further threats, then I will call the police and I will spill the dirt on you with consequences which I can only leave you to imagine."

JJ responded with a disparaging laugh: *"Fine words! But you are not in any position to harm me, whereas I can and will, harm you."*

"*And those are brave words from* **you**, *but they don't take into account that I have, from Tony, everything there is to know about you and I will not hesitate to make sure that that information finds its way into the hands of whatever authorities may be interested in stopping you in your tracks. I have left instructions that should anything happen to me then that information will come out of hiding. And now I am afraid your time is up.*"

With that she left the coffee shop and took a taxi back to her flat. In the cab, she opened her bag and turned off her tape recorder. If it served no other purpose, the recording would be the best way to inform Alice of exactly what had just happened and to discourage any further approach from JJ once he was made aware of it.

A week later and true to her word, Alice called Sally from Manchester airport to say that she had not forgotten about the trip to London the following day and asked what train they would be catching. She also wanted to know what it was all about, but Sally said she would explain everything the following day on the train – it was too late in the evening for Sally to explain now.

As soon as they boarded the train to London the following morning they settled down to talk.

Sally started by referring to her encounter the previous week with JJ and she played the recording to Alice, who was impressed with the way Sally had handled herself, saying that she had been very convincing. Sally did not want to take up too much time on JJ. She moved on quickly to explain why they were going to London, showing Alice the correspondence she had received from HMRC. Alice, stony-faced, read it slowly and carefully. Sally had previously been too ashamed to tell Alice the whole story, and so she explained that she had unwittingly helped Tony to profit, illegally, from insider dealings in shares.

Alice told Sally that she should request from Miss Channing copies of the six letters stolen from her flat and Sally felt stupid for not having asked for these weeks ago.

Over coffee, they discussed tactics and Alice agreed that Sally's plan to be completely frank with Miss Channing was the only way forward.

Sally told Alice the little she knew about the mysterious overseas bank account. They talked about Sally possibly representing to Miss Channing that she knew nothing of that account but thought that it would involve too large a risk when Sally need not take any.

They thought, on balance, that it would be sensible for Sally to volunteer her involvement with MI5 in case Miss Channing was already aware of it. Of course, it was impossible to know what information HMRC had received, but if Tony was the informant, then the MI5 connection was something he might well have revealed to the tax authorities and by referring to it herself, Sally thought she would be demonstrating to Miss Channing that she was not hiding anything.

Their discussions on the 10:15 to London Euston led to few conclusions, but it was so comforting for Sally to have someone to talk to, to share her gnawing worries.

That was until they reached Reading, when Alice disclosed a tumultuous piece of news which jolted Sally as if the train had run into the buffers.

"Sally, there is something important I haven't yet told you. This is so difficult for me because I know I should have said something to you much earlier, but I had hoped it wouldn't be necessary."

"What's that?"

"I'll explain. Last year your Tony wrote to me pleading with me not to tell you that he had placed $50,000 into a bank account in Zurich in your name. He said he had done so because he knew he had badly let you

*down and he felt very guilty that you could not practice as a solicitor after all your years of study and training. It was hardly compensation, he said, but it was all he could do. He said that it wouldn't be sensible if he told **you** about this – firstly, he knew that you would refuse the money; secondly, if his colleagues found out about the money they would think that you were aware of the whereabouts of what he called 'a larger sum' and would target you; and, lastly, the amount was intended to help you in the event you needed something 'for a rainy day'. None of this made much sense to me, but I saw no harm in going along with it at the time and I planned, in a few years' time, to reveal the existence of the account to you."*

Before Sally, open-mouthed, could say anything to Alice in response, the train had arrived at Euston – only just avoiding the buffers.

They got to HMRC just in time not to be late. Sally and Alice were immediately ushered into an unattractive basement meeting room distempered in lettuce green. A thirty-something year old, bespectacled Miss Channing and her colleague, Peter Anderton-Smythe, joined them a few minutes later. Introductions were made, and Sally was cautioned.

"Before we proceed," announced Miss Channing, *"is there anything, Miss Bridge, you want to tell us?"*

"Yes. Firstly, I want to apologise again for the discourtesy in not replying to your initial letters. This was borne entirely of the belief, without even opening them, that the letters were merely circulars and did not contain anything of any importance. I am taxed on a PAYE basis and always have been and I didn't, for one minute, think they contained anything of significance. I know that was stupid of me. When I spoke to you, Miss Channing, on 22nd August, I explained that I had no idea of anything I might have done which could possibly have involved fraud. That remains completely true, however, I have since then become aware of circumstances which may well be the reason for your investigation. Please let me please explain the background …"

And Sally set out the facts, yet again, of how she had been recruited by the security services and duped by one of its agents. She explained how she had come to be excluded from the legal profession but exonerated from any involvement in insider dealing or fraud. Sally went on to explain that it was not until last week that she had found out what Miss Channing meant when she referred to a bank account in Sally's name.

"I can assure you that I had no previous knowledge of this account, which is why when you and I spoke on the telephone again on 26th August I was so certain that there could be no basis for HMRC pursuing me. If you need her to, my sister can corroborate that. I would like to emphasise that I have never had any source of cash from which I could have transferred funds into any account and none of the moneys that may be in it come from me. I have been working in a supermarket and my only other job was, for a short period, working as a trainee solicitor. When both of our parents died in August 2014, we received moneys from their estate and this cash is still in my Lloyds bank account in Oldham, no part of which, as my bank statements will show, have I moved anywhere – let alone abroad. In fact, I have been abroad only once in my life. I can't see how I might fit the stereotype of an international tax evader."

Miss Channing asked several questions to seek to clarify Sally's exposition.

"Have you ever taken any money out of the overseas bank account?"

"No, I have not."

Miss Channing and her colleague glanced at each other – a glance which Alice noticed. She sensed what was happening and just as Miss Channing was preparing to ask Sally another question, Alice jumped in with something staggering – staggering to Sally, that is.

*"But **I** have,"* said Alice, *"would you please allow me to explain?"*

Miss Channing merely nodded. Sally did not know what to say and merely registered with some annoyance the fact that Alice was supposed to be attending the meeting to hold Sally's hand – not to hold court.

Alice continued. *"Firstly, I can confirm that Tony Forth told me about the bank account in August last year, but that I didn't tell Sally anything about it until this morning when she first spoke to me about your enquiries. I held that information back from Sally because I had stupidly promised Tony Forth that I would not mention it, and I could see no harm in that. I planned to tell Sally about the existence of the account in a few years' time when she had got over the trauma of all that has happened in her life."*

Alice went on in some detail, explaining how she had taken $45,000 out of the account. She emphasised that she had done so without Sally knowing. She showed Miss Channing a receipt from the hotel where she had stayed in Zurich in a single room. Alice finished by saying how ashamed she was of what she had done but added that she had months ago repaid the whole $45,000 back into the account. She added that she had known nothing of the illegal insider dealing scam carried out by Tony Forth – she had found out about that only today.

"There seems to be much that you two sisters have been keeping from each other," said Miss Channing with a wry smile.

The otherwise inscrutable Miss Channing asked her colleague whether he had anything further to ask and when he shook his head, the hour-long meeting was declared at an end. Miss Channing would write to Sally with the next step and send her copies of the six missing letters.

Sally and Alice took the train back to Manchester together. They were exhausted and did not want to talk, however, that was the one thing they were impelled to do as soon as they boarded the train.

Suffused, as she then was, with a toxic mix of impatience, irritation and anger, Sally, while she was waiting for Alice to get coffee, thought that she might be about to explode. So angry was she that as soon as Alice had returned Sally could not hold back.

"I really don't understand what's happening. For more than a year you have withheld telling me about the existence of this damned bank account; then right at the end of our train journey this morning you reveal what happened with Tony Forth so that we wouldn't have time to discuss it before the most important meeting I will ever attend. Then without any warning you let loose a bombshell at the meeting itself that you stole $45,000 from the account. How could you possibly hide all this from me when you know that my being able to prove my innocence may well depend on it? I feel that you are trying to sabotage me!"

"I will explain everything to you as best I can," replied Alice, sipping her coffee, with eyes looking down with more than a hint of contrition.

"All this is deeply mortifying to me and I owe you an endless apology. I have already explained to you why I held back from telling you of the existence of the bank account. I can see why you might not want to accept my explanation, but I assure you that I thought my inaction was in your best interests. As regards my taking the $45,000 … you see, my business was suffering a temporary but crucial cash shortage that would have seen the end of the company and so I 'borrowed' the money from your account with the aim of paying it all back very quickly and, as I said, I have already repaid the whole $45,000."

Sally was too startled to be able to say anything.

"I am not at all proud of any of this. You'll remember the time earlier this year when I had a meeting in Munich. Well, that is when I took your passport, went from there to Zurich and drew out the $45,000 which the company was desperate for. It was easy and too tempting an opportunity to miss. I had hoped that you wouldn't ever have got to know about the withdrawal. I am so ashamed. I know it was utterly foolish and what's more it seems that it has led to our current crisis with the tax authorities."

At that, Sally could restrain herself no longer.

"What do you mean 'our' crisis? It is me who is the one being prosecuted."

"But I am now also in the firing line because by taking that money and telling HMRC, I, too, could be prosecuted for money laundering if the $50,000 put into the account was from Tony's fraud. Sally, we are in this together and, if we are to get out of it, we will need to work together."

"But if you had immediately explained to me that Tony had spoken to you then, I wouldn't be in this bloody state in the first place! How could you have

thought that it was right to withhold any of that information from me?"

"Well, I am sorry ..."

"That's not good enough!" Sally exclaimed; and it was as well that the carriage was almost empty because she had begun to shout loudly.

"What I would really like you to explain to me," Sally continued with heightened intensity, *"is how you could have delayed giving me all this vital information. You didn't tell me of the existence of the account; you didn't tell me that it came from Tony Forth; nor that you stole from the account – none of it – until today, **until today!** And you have divulged it, reluctantly and in instalments as if it was some TV drama. It's not! ... it's my life. I can't understand what the hell you have been playing at! And why did you wait for the interview before telling me? You must have been thinking about it because otherwise you wouldn't have brought that hotel receipt with you – or do you take it with you wherever you go in case you might need it for some reason?"*

There was then a short pause – a pause for breath for Sally and a pause for Alice to get some respite.

"And how could you possibly have thought that keeping your word to Tony Forth was more important

than keeping faith with your sister. Had you told me earlier, I wouldn't have suffered the angst I am now feeling! I would have got rid of the money immediately."

"Maybe it **was** the wrong decision," replied Alice, *"but I made it in what I thought was your best interests."*

"You keep on saying 'MY' best interests, but don't you really mean 'yours'? If you had told me about the bank account when you should have done then you would not have been able to take that $45,000 from the account. That's why you didn't tell me! Isn't that it?"

"That's utter nonsense! I have already told you that it was to protect you from Tony Forth's henchmen."

"But not protection from you stealing the money! You have behaved totally selfishly! And another thing – tell me why you felt it necessary to tell Channing that you had taken funds out of the bank account?"

Any sister faced with a tirade such as this would have folded – sentences ago. But not Alice. Now it was her turn to show anger.

"You might not have noticed" replied Alice, *"but it seemed very clear to me that Channing **knew** that the $45,000 had been withdrawn and if that's correct then HMRC must have known that a person called 'Sally Bridge' had been the person who had withdrawn it. Had I not spoken up, they would not have believed anything*

you told them! After all the things I have done for you, how can you possibly think that I have acted selfishly?"

"OK, so you did get me my birth certificate, for which I will always be grateful, but you were not exactly depriving yourself when you went on your travels to Turkey!"

"That's effing unkind. Would you like to stop there so you can calm down before you say something else you will really regret?"

"No! I **haven't** finished. I am **so** furious with you. Time and time again when I think back, even to our youth, you have put yourself first and it's only now that I am beginning to see you for what you are."

"What **are** you talking about, Sally?"

"OK, I wasn't going to say this, but since you ask … when we were kids you always lorded it over me as the elder sister, getting me to run your errands and fetch things for you; you ruined our ballet birthday outing when we were 14 by sulking over the fact that you really wanted to be with our next-door neighbour instead; and … you went off to Quimper without me; and you used blackmail to get me to cheat for you in your maths exam! Will **that** be enough for you?"

"I can't believe you're dredging up events from the distant past and expecting me to take you seriously. I had no idea that these thoughts might be festering in *your little head. You definitely need help. I have always been a loving sister to you, as you have been to me, and your outburst is sheer madness. I know I was wrong not telling you about the bank account and taking that money, but I have apologised."*

"Repeating that doesn't ..."

*"Let me finish, Sally! I have listened enough to you. None of the many things **you** have done which have hurt **me**, unwittingly or not, have affected my love and admiration for you and it upsets me to the core to think that you obviously don't feel anywhere near the same way towards me – and haven't for a long time; perhaps ever."*

*"And what, pray, have I done to injure **you**?"*

*"Do you really think that you are blameless in all this, **do** you?"*

There was a short pause and Alice continued.

"Maybe you do, but I am not going to resort to the kind of baseless vindictiveness that you have just shown!"

They arrived in Manchester Victoria broken vessels, each making her way home separately even though they lived next door to each other; each numbed, exhausted and unable to eat, drink or sleep.

It had taken less than 12 hours for them to demolish a relationship which had been 30 years in the making, a relationship which neither of them could have imagined was as fragile and as flimsy as it had now shown itself to be.

Sally and Alice both realised that there could be no going back. They would replay the day's events in their minds on countless occasions and the outcome would always be the same.

33.

POSTSCRIPT

The first thing Sally recognised was the handwriting on the envelope.

She saw that it had been posted three days earlier and bore a second-class stamp franked in Oldham. Sally knew that Alice was in residence next door because she had heard her radio, and she asked herself why she had not simply slipped the envelope through her letterbox.

Even before she had opened the envelope, Sally realised what it was that Alice was telling her by using the post. Alice was making a point. By choosing not to slip it through Sally's door, she was telling her that their physical proximity had no meaning to her and that they were now as distant from each other as the postal system could possibly accommodate. By using a second-class stamp, Alice was telling her that she was no longer a priority.

Dear Sally

So, after almost 30 years of twinship, it has now come to this - the disintegration of our relationship.

I was utterly astounded at your outburst on Wednesday and quite frankly I was not able to take it. On reflection, I see that there are two main reasons for that.

Firstly, I wasn't able to face up to your scathing criticism of my failure to tell you of the bank account. I will certainly admit that I think that your criticism is justified, although that doesn't make it any easier for me to accept. It is hard to admit guilt like this to oneself let alone to someone else - particularly one's twin sister - and I could not listen to any more from you, particularly since you were obviously unwilling to accept that what I did I did sincerely, believing that I was helping you.

It is a cruel and completely unjustified accusation that I hid the bank account from you only so that I could rob you. Stealing money from the account was the worst thing I have ever done and it was not in my mind when I determined to keep the existence of the account from you. Surely you can accept that my repaying the money back into the bank account so quickly proves this.

But there is something else which I have held back from you and in an effort to get you to forgive me, I must disclose something I originally vowed to myself that I would never tell you. If I am apologising to you for hiding the bank account from you (as I am), then it would not be right for me to keep anything else back from you.

I was always pleading with you to introduce me to Simon, but that became somewhat disingenuous because I had already met him.

In telling you about this, I appreciate that I may be putting even more distance between us and that you will hate me even more. However, I don't feel I have any choice.

It must have been about a year ago. I was watching television in our room at the hotel one evening. I can't remember where you were. There was a knock at the bedroom door, and I stupidly opened it without looking. It was Simon, although I had no idea who it was until he introduced himself and explained that he was passing by and came to say hello to you. Well, I invited him in - what else could I do? We chatted about nothing in particular. He rambled a lot. He had obviously been drinking. He said he knew all about me and was pleased to meet me at last. He asked me a lot of questions about you (which I remember offended me at the time) and he suddenly became a bit too familiar; he touched my face - twice. I was quite frightened and asked him to leave. He saw how upset I was, and he apologised and left immediately.

I didn't know what to do. If I had then told you what had happened, I knew that that might affect your job. Had I told you later on, I knew that it would affect your relationship with him. I didn't think that I had the right to do either of those things. I felt that to say nothing was also wrong, but I took the coward's way out and decided to keep my mouth shut - that is, until now because I know that he no longer means anything to you. So now you know.

I said there were two reasons I went off on Wednesday without confronting you properly as I should have done. The second reason was that I was dumbfounded that you should think that I have always acted selfishly towards you. I wanted to stand my ground on this, but I am not good at confrontation or marshalling my thoughts on the spur of the moment in the same way as you are.

It defies belief that you can say that I have been selfish when everything points in the opposite direction. Having thought about this since Wednesday, I still can't understand how you can possibly believe I behaved selfishly when I spent months in Turkey sorting out your birth certificate. I went off to an alien environment on my own with nowhere to stay, with limited resources, no contacts and no knowledge of Turkish. I had no idea what I should be doing to solve your problem. I didn't know how long it would take and yet I stuck it out and eventually dealt with it very effectively and for one reason only and that was because I made a promise to you in the knowledge that you really did have a serious problem - and one that was not of my making.

Do you really think that was being selfish? If there was any selfishness in my having to stay in Turkey, maybe it was on your part!

When you were trying to work out how to tackle the problem you have with the tax prosecution, I immediately dropped everything I had planned to do on my first day back in order to give you every bit of help you needed; and I went with you to London.

Not only that. I was prepared to admit to the authorities that I had stolen money from you and I did so for one reason, which was to ensure that your answers appeared consistent and believable.

As a result, I have stabbed myself in the back in order to get you off the hook. How can I have been so foolish as to have done such a thing for you?

As I write this letter, another example occurs to me. There are probably scores more.

Do you think that I wanted to share a room with you at the hotel for so long? I did so only because you were at your lowest and someone needed to be with you. I didn't tell you, but I had been offered my own bedsit by someone at work and I turned it down for you!

How ridiculous you are to accuse me of being selfish. You have inexplicably got it all the wrong way round. Sally, what has happened?

The spats you mentioned when we were kids are too far back in history to expect that we should have the same recollections - and we certainly do not!

For one, you said that I used to bully you into running errands for me, but that is the spin you put on it. You have conveniently forgotten that each time you did something for me you insisted that I had to reciprocate! Step back for a minute and think. I clearly remember when I asked you to tell lies to Ma to cover up my getting into trouble at school - I think it was something to do with homework - you agreed to do so but only if I gave you my new plaid skirt - the one that I loved so much and which had cost me more than anything else I'd ever bought.

And the ballet outing! That awful day! Although I had a crush on Brian next door, I was happy to go to the ballet and said as much when we had our family discussion.

You've also got it completely back to front on Quimper. It was Ma who insisted I go without you. In fact, I went to her in tears, pleading with her not to force me to go without you, because I knew how distraught you'd be; however, she was adamant because she thought that I would otherwise fall even further back in French - she said you would be all right and she asked me not to discuss any of this with you.

And there's another much later episode - the one with grandma's house in Lowca, when you thought I had plied Ma and grandma with drugs or had brain-washed them, or I don't know what, to ensure that Lowca went to me alone! Again, you were utterly deluding yourself. I had no influence in any of this, and even if I did, do you think that I would have tried to manipulate things so that I would inherit Lowca (or anything) from grandma without you having your half? That is just one more example of you jumping to a completely wrong conclusion about me.

I'll mention one other episode - the maths test. Again, your recollection is totally different from mine, since it was your idea in the first place because you thought it would be a bit of excitement. I did encourage you, yes, because it suited me to, but to say I blackmailed you is utter rubbish! I would have been in more trouble at school than you if we'd been found out!

I have made mistakes and so have you. If we were to stack them in two piles - yours and mine - it would be impossible to work out which pile was higher. You should know that full well, and it is precisely because of that that I am so hurt. If your outburst on the train was of the moment that is one thing; but if it was the build-up of a lifetime's resentment of me - that is something I could not live with. Either way, I deserve an apology from you!

Alice

34.
AFTERWORDS

Although this is a tale of persecution, of loss of identity, mistakes, misunderstandings, deception, bad decisions and of many other such doom-laden occurrences, none of them would have a monopoly on the fortunes of our players, as those who may be curious can see below. Sometimes an author's characters manage to take on a life of their own which the pen cannot control nor the keyboard influence.

Brian still lives with his parents next door to where the Bridge family lived in Ashton-under-Lyne and he is the manager of an ice-skating rink in Manchester.

Rhianne lectures on the English Language at the University of Bangor.

Doreen Okanwe is a senior judge in the Federal High Court of Nigeria.

Tony is still in prison in the Cayman Islands.

JJ never did make any further contact with Sally, and no one knows what happened to Alex Carstairs or the girl with the pink hair.

Rita's son, Tom, still lives in Lowca, now in his mother's old house, with his wife and three children, just a few doors up from where the Imbers used to live.

Mr Chambers retired and moved from Ashton-under-Lyne to Lowca with his wife.

Cedric works as an estate agent in Manchester.

Ben Ashcrofte is working as a family solicitor in a two-partner practice in Balham, South London.

Yusef lives in Turkey and is an English teacher at a prestigious high school.

Mrs Tarkani is still working at Lidburys of Oldham and remains a good friend of Sally.

Simon Leigh continues to be the Manager of Lidburys, Heaton Park. He never did spot the kisses in Sally's reports.

Every Lidburys store now employs a 'Front of House', a position which is accorded a salary level equivalent to that of Manager.

Although the close friendship between Rosemary and Sally is no longer, they do occasionally meet in the coffee shop at Lidburys of Oldham.

In due course, a Mr Keith Weed became the president of the Royal Horticultural Society.

After three months, HMRC dropped all claims against Sally since there was no evidence of fraud on her part. She would merely need to pay tax on the interest arising on the Zurich bank account.

No claim was ever pursued against Alice for taking the $45,000.

Alice continues to run her travel agency. She has been very successful and travels the world – but on her own.

And as for Sally herself? She continues to play snakes and ladders but is slowly getting better dice.

However close the twins had been, there were so many occasions when their foundation had suffered damage and developed cracks, to the point where, had they been brave enough to examine them thoroughly, Sally and Alice might have concluded that the edifice must have been doomed. Yet this was not an inevitable conclusion since it would not have taken much for Sally, the prime antagonist, to have been able to 'paper over the cracks', 'bite her lip' and recognise that, in every family, mistakes are made which, if capable of being quantified, would show an equal volume of justified rancour on each side of the fence.

However, Sally never did reply to Alice's hand-written letter seeking an apology. She did not even acknowledge it. Their wounds were too deep, and it is not surprising that they failed to re-establish anything near the closeness which they had previously enjoyed.

It was fortunate that Sally and Alice had remained neighbours because that was the means by which they could – if only as members of polite society rather than as the only surviving members of the Bridge family – gradually resume perfunctory conversations with each other, as it were, 'over the garden fence'.

Despite the inability of Sally and Alice to reconstruct their twinship (as Alice referred to it) they did manage to carry out a partial reconditioning of it sufficient to enable them to get together to talk about their grandparents and their parents and to light candles in their remembrance once each year on Tisha B'Av – because that was the day on which each of them had died.

Printed in Great Britain
by Amazon